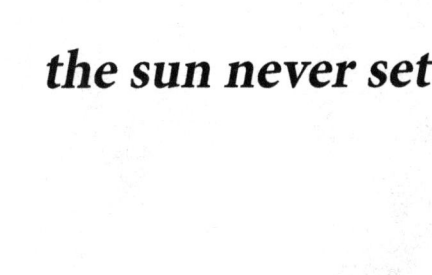

the sun never set

Also by Christopher M. Struck

Kennig & Gold

*8: A Song for the Peach Tree
in My Master's Garden*

the sun never set
a novel

Christopher M. Struck

Livonia, Michigan

THE SUN NEVER SET

This book is a work of fiction. The characters, incidents, and dialogue are drawn from the author's imagination and are not to be construed as real. Any resemblance to actual events or persons, living or dead, is entirely coincidental.

Published by BHC Press

Library of Congress Control Number: 2021944524

ISBN Numbers:
978-1-64397-280-0 (Hardcover)
978-1-64397-281-7 (Softcover)
978-1-64397-282-4 (Ebook)

For information, write:
BHC Press
885 Penniman #5505
Plymouth, MI 48170

Visit the publisher:
www.bhcpress.com

Thank you to all the international students and people,
who shared the spring of 2013 in Bangkok.

Author's Note

Jake, the main character of this story, and the many people he meets on his journey are fictional but grounded in reality. The general circumstances and places exist or existed, for the most part, as described. *The Sun Never Set*, tells the fictional tale of a lost love from a spring in Thailand, when the hopes of youth were high and cultures from across the world collided, much like myself and others, from all over the world, when we chased our imaginations and discovered ourselves during the hot nights of Bangkok while studying abroad by day.

Bangkok is a beautiful, lively city with breathtaking sights by day and by night. Only a few years ago, Bangkok's night life had no curfew, military or otherwise. Even before the pandemic and while I lived in Thailand in 2013, a curfew was gradually enforced, earlier and earlier, closing clubs before they even really opened to their clientele. Most nights were simple nights out with friends and most of the time, we spent hanging out with and meeting expatriates from around the world in clubs and lounges of all kinds, sipping wine and buying bottles for dimes. We dressed to the nines and had a good time, and for that and all of the beauty of the city of Bangkok, I hope the world changes for the better.

So with that short introduction, let me tell you a tale set in Bangkok, a city of lights, a city that truly never slept, a sprawling metropolis filled with towers of gold, ivory and steel, a tropical paradise of avenues filled with towering trees, and boulevards decorated with delicate flowers, and most of all, a city filled with people from all over the world who dreamed.

the sun never set

chapter one

The French

Our motorbikes cut between cars, fighting for space as the road narrowed, forming a long line amongst other bikes, ducking between taillights and headlights. One by one we flew onto the bridge, and up toward the elevated highway that narrowed still further as it approached the red horizon. At the last second, an exit peeled off and our motorbikes ducked out and away from the death trap. They were not allowed there. The wind was in our hair with the stench of shit from the gutters and of the sweat caked on our drivers. My hands held the polished, chrome grips at the edges of my seat, and I blinked, trying to keep my eyes on the road as the sun faded away and the night rose into full color.

I looked over at the other bikes to see the French guys and girls, in some cases two to a bike, following close behind me. Streetlights lit our way as our motorbikes weaved beneath and away from the highway. We found the roads were well paved and kept good, but disorganized.

The dark, black asphalt gleamed and sparkled under the low sun and headlights of our motorbikes, swarming through the canal-like pathways in a myriad of colorful, faded neon that caught stray light and flashed brightly. I would learn later that long rides in Bangkok were dangerous, and I would stop taking them after seeing the road rash and broken bones of a few of my classmates. Cabs were cheaper anyway, but the feel of the wind in your hair against the high humidity was like sailing out into the ocean on a hot summer day. The wind was at your back and the sun on your shoulders just the same.

We had it good. We had it made. We came upon Khao San Road as if it was just another byway. After we had paid our hundred baht and walked along the side soi, we saw Khao San grow out and open into a long stretch full of shops, street food, and people like us. Young and hopeful. Interested and happy. We wanted so much to believe in the good of the world.

We all led and followed each other as we dispersed among the aisles and racks of dollar shirts and foot massages. The heat of the final sun beat down much softer than that of the late afternoon, and we sunk into it comfortably like flowers bending in a spring breeze. The road was longer than we could see, and it took us a while to get anywhere because the girls would stop at each shop only to browse.

The girls were French, which seemed to mean they took more time to carefully examine anything they did not want to buy. Since two of them were my roommates, I felt a need to stick around rather than further explore the caverns of this exotic abyss. Yes, two French girls were my roommates. Maeva and Valerie. Both beautiful and in love with the heat. They had dark, tanned skin from French islands in the Caribbean, but smooth hair and silky smiles like the French girls of one's dreams. They spoke in heavy English that sounded sweet and rhythmical. If they had felt the same about my French, I might have learned to say more than *Je n'compris*.

The crowd thickened as we drifted along with the other pockets of people on the long, straight road. Its straightness gave it a certain austerity. We all just passed through. It stayed. Locals weaved between us like they had seen it all before, and they had. Even if we felt powerful in our fleeting taste of foreign fruit, we were just passengers.

The Thai vendors carried insects on trays. Little toys meant for breaking. My favorite salesmen were the little girls peddling roses and asking me to buy one for the young women in our group. If I didn't want a rose, they called after me to bet a hundred baht on a game of thumb war. One of the many nights on Khao San, I'd put them to the test and lose my money, but tonight we merely wandered past.

At the center of the road stood two bars that pumped club music into the street. They were usually packed even in the middle of the day, but we got lucky. Both bars stood mostly empty, and our group of eight took a table at the one on the right. I sat across from Maeva who smiled at me with her shy eyelashes fluttering in the glow of the dim lights that hung along the open-air entrance to the dive.

Forevermore I would long to be back in that moment when she looked at me with those eyes. I wonder now if I would recognize something more in them than I had then. But, we would sit back and fall into the roles that we played for others. We would lose what might have been in the naïve hope that the world would stay the same.

Four-liter towers of beer were taken out for us, and we drank. We laughed and talked, too, but mostly, we drank. We filled little plastic cups, pulling round after round from the beer towers as if we had our own private tap. Above all, the advantage that Khao San had, was that its beer towers and beach bucket pails of mixed drinks were cheap. And as we sat, drinking, the tables filling around us, we had all the time in the world. The Thai insect vendors would stop at each table and show scorpions. A few days later, I'd come back with the Germans and eat one. To-night, we waved them off and simply talked. I mostly listened, since French was the main tongue of the table.

The group would leave me alone at the table to smoke ciga-rettes and then come back. I think almost all of the French kids smoked. One of those bogus eighty-twenty rules, but it gave me time to reflect. To stare into the bubbling, gold liquid that slid down my throat with such regular ease.

They came back, and talk resumed as if nothing had bro-ken it. They tried to keep me in the conversation even during the French parts, but I was often the nervous sort and hadn't worked up the courage, liquid or otherwise, yet. Eventually, Maeva stood up and went to a waiter. We all knew what she was asking for: Salsa or Spanish music. Whichever they could play. When it came on, Valerie joined her, and Maeva motioned for me to dance, too.

I stood, my serious mood bent by the Chang beer, and joined her. She smiled at me in that same shy way as she twisted forward and back to the sensual tune of the music. I wanted to pull her close, to taste her, but I had my convictions about keep-ing things among roommates professional, so we merely danced.

Others joined us, and I danced eye to eye with Monique. I didn't know if she was single. The song's beat kept our hearts in that youthful place of hope where the stark reality of chasing nothing couldn't bear down on our old souls.

We lost our time as the night slipped in on us without warn-ing. Our bar and the other across the street had filled complete-ly with backpackers and foreigners in crisp shirts, and I guessed that's how nightlife worked in Bangkok. It had been our turn to start the night, and we had started it.

Maeva ran her hand down my back along my spine. I turned and fell into her eyes, sweet but dangerous, like a glass of red wine. I pulled her into me and let the passion of the song take us to another place where the cares of our faraway world did not affect us.

Our hips interlocked and our lips almost followed. Her pleated skirt flirted with my jeans until I was pulled away by Valerie, and the world swam back.

I would never forget the way that Maeva looked at me.

But she wasn't the only one to cast that look.

Perhaps that is how it always began.

Or as I decided later, the next woman to cast that accidental smile, knew perfectly well what it meant to drop her eyes and lift them with the curve of her lips.

Mischa. I'd meet her soon enough. Like a phantom of the future hung out to break all the hearts of the men at Nonsi Residence.

On that night, we, the French and I, and all the rest, stood amongst those lucky ones who descended upon Bangkok in a mythical spring while we still could.

I walked upright with a confident grin, knowing that we were de facto kings of a rare sliver of gold in an open world. Or so I thought. Even in those first moments, the fates began to build against me. Meeting Mischa was only the beginning of the sequence of events of my fall.

• • •

Studying abroad always comes with challenges, which may cancel the whole experience before it begins. For me, after a series of lucky coincidences, I booked a last-minute flight for January 2nd, but kept my New Year's plans. The day before setting out on the fated adventure to Bangkok, I came home on January 1st at 3 a.m. with enough rum and Coke in me to have lost most of the night to time.

No matter how hung over I was though, I was at O'Hare mid-morning the next day for the first leg of the trip to Bangkok. We flew into San Francisco, coming in under a dense cloud of fog. I spent the night next to the ticket counters with my life packed into two duffel bags, a backpack, and one fifties-style suitcase.

On the flight to Hong Kong, still hung over and even more tired, I met a talkative, old guy. Upon hearing that I was going to Bangkok, he brightened and slapped his little airplane table about as hard as he could. "Bangkok! You're going to Bangkok?

"Yeah."

"Well, just remember when you're there, don't hesitate. You've got to bring the hammer down."

I turned my head slowly to look directly at him. "Bring what?"

He said it again with more emphasis. "You've got to bring the hammer down!"

After the layover in Hong Kong, I was finally on my way to Bangkok. I wasn't sure what he meant at the time, and I'm not sure I lived up to his expectations. I certainly didn't know what to expect.

Truth be told, when I arrived after fifty-four hours in transit at 12:30 a.m. on a Saturday morning, I didn't expect anyone to be up, but I should have. Just about any night could run much later.

I paid almost fourteen hundred baht (or fifty dollars) for a Benz taxi that got lost on the way to Nonsi, and I had to give him directions from my phone, causing an exorbitant amount of international roaming in the time before flat rates.

We arrived at the dark beige building, Nonsi, hidden behind a high, yellow-brick wall with no more pomp than one of the stray dogs fighting off cockroaches for scraps in the trash. The patio and office were quiet, the office being shut behind steel. A security guard helped me with my bags to the lobby where I waited as the guards checked my ID against the list of late-night check-ins. For a moment, I looked away from their command center and saw her arrive.

Mischa.

Confident and quiet, the half-Japanese, half-Russian, American-born woman of my dreams slipped into the corner of my eye. She took in the night like she belonged to it. Dressed in a loose white shirt and still wearing a sun hat in the middle of the night, she eased through the glass doors of the lobby with no more regard for me than a statue might have for a snail.

Of course, I looked at her. Gawked is more like it. First through the glass where I knew that she saw me. And the second time when she had entered. I couldn't help but size her up. She was a lily in a garden of thorns. I could have told a friend across a table on any day before then that she was the woman I would have thought up if I could.

She hovered. Her eyelashes fluttered. She looked down, smirked, and blushed as her eyes caught mine in a moment of pure mystery. My heart was gone.

"This way please," the guard said. He escorted me to my room where I would meet Maeva and Valerie, but there was only the girl I had seen on my mind. More than anything, she would hold my thoughts captive— Mischa.

Who was the girl in white? That lady of the night? I'd meet her soon enough, I knew. The weeks between were torture as I caught glimpses of her passing through the other doors to the tower opposite mine. Leaving the pool just before I'd arrive.

What the truth was, I could never know, but I could build up the romance of it all in my hopes. Maybe my hopes were too high?

But then again, maybe not.

In the meantime, there were many other ways to occupy one's time in Bangkok.

• • •

I opened the door to the lobby and heard the magnetic click of the lock behind me. A fresh blast from the air conditioner wafted over me like I was cocooned in a frozen blanket.

The cold relieved me. We didn't turn our air conditioning on in our apartment. The heat would become so intense that I slept with the windows open most nights, stark naked with a thin sheet for privacy's sake. The lobby was bare, save for two identical sets of couches and a chair around a long, glass coffee table. Often, you'd find a couple people there just waiting, like now.

Monique reclined in the armchair with her long legs crossed and skin shining. She had an authoritatively sophisticated air and a crimp smirk that hardly registered on the Richter scale of lip movements.

I joined her with my oft-called charming Wisconsin smile. She stood and kissed my cheek. I kissed the air beside her and hugged her strongly with one arm.

She didn't talk after that. I always wondered how to pry into her mind. It strikes me now that she may have been nervous or concerned about her English, but she had a tasteful look that spoke volumes about her presence of mind. It kept me from being aggressive despite her beauty, but I did enjoy our brief conversations when they occurred. She never really spoke much, even in French, so I guess she preferred to keep to herself.

Maeva and Valerie joined us, laughing as always. We still needed Hugo, and I think Madeline, and Jacques, before we left for the restaurant. It was either them or one of the many groups of French girls who lived at Nonsi. We waited together in the quiet glimmer of pink light that drifted through the floor-to-ceiling window of the lobby.

Hugo came at last and, once the group had finished kissing cheeks, we set off for a small bar up the road toward Rama IV along the train tracks.

We came along the low wall around Nonsi and started off to the right past the security desk. It had been converted into a street restaurant, but before we went there, we wanted to explore the area around our building a little further.

Sitting out along the wall opposite Nonsi, waiting for a sale, was the collection of motorbike riders who had once taken us to Khao San. Usually five or so, and they liked to laugh with each other. They rarely did much else but eat colorful fruit from a vendor that made daily appearances in front of our apartments.

We passed them with short nods and lazily made it along the hot, black asphalt past the gray walls of the surrounding buildings. Nonsi was one of the few outliers amongst the cement that fenced in the properties in our district, Khlong Toei.

Khlong Toei. You mention that to a child of Bangkok's upper crust, and they'll tell you it's rough shit. The ghetto.

It is, in a way, especially when you think of the monstrous meat market and the area around it. But we were quite literally on the other side of the tracks from that, where the decrepit and complete projects of princes and the nouveau riche lay behind two feet thick sloped walls of cement. The princely mansions and the dilapidated buildings were equally vacant and lived in. Some were lived in by the rich and the decrepit were squatted in by the poor—though many of each were vacant.

As we passed a street restaurant on the left, you could see the disparity. The cement wall had been broken away in a circle, and the dormant skeleton of a four-story house sat blackening and exposed to the constant humidity, beating sun, and torrential rain. I learned later that the operators of the street restaurant had broken the hole in the wall to squat there. On that day, I caught the sight of chickens through the tall grass kept only by a long, thick rope tied to their ankles. Even the hollowed out and blackened, forgotten ruins of a prince's project had become someone else's home while the mansion on the other side of the walls beside it remained quiet most of the year.

We took a right at the intersection and passed down our soi to Chua Phloeng, the main road along the train tracks and the hardest thing to pronounce in the Thai language. There, we walked past a few more apartment buildings until we came to two actual restaurants with outdoor seating that had set up shop beside each other. The highway exit was just up ahead, but all we could see was the overpass and a car graveyard that wove its way beneath it.

I never did see anything human in there, but the rusted carcasses of the crushed cars, fenced in and forgotten, were a sordid sight.

We entered one of the empty restaurants. Despite their appearance of unpopularity, these restaurants often attracted all sorts of gentry that would park their cars, shiny new BMWs and Nissans, along the side of the road.

Tonight, it was just us and a loud group of four in the corner chatting it up with exaggerated bursts of laughter. Long strings of big, incandescent light bulbs were strung from the walls along the outer edge of the open seating area to a tower at the center like white spindles of a large wheel.

We took a table near the center of the square, and we ordered what we considered to be adventurous. Even in Bangkok, the typical menu tended to be less than truly exotic. Only the language changed. The actual palette required few alterations from its typical formula. And many dishes could only be found in the homes of our more affluent classmates.

Still, we felt, each on our own, the sense that we were making some dramatic shift into a new world by making this truly small sacrifice of our normalcy. That's what it all was in the end. The sacrifice of our normal for a false sense of growth.

In that same token, we all came first as merely interlopers until those foreign things became ordinary. On this night, we sat around a white metal table in matching chairs that could've been picked out of a 90s American catalogue.

The meal was cheap but within the context of Bangkok, still overpriced. I can't speak for the others, but I'd never come back. Most likely because my standards would adapt to a cleanish kitchen whether or not the restaurant had walls. It was only important to know how things were being made if you wanted to avoid any surprises.

This wasn't New York where restaurants have ratings on the door that represent the cleanliness of the kitchen. In Thailand, Thai food was, for the most part, either eaten in homes or on the streets. The best Thai restaurant that I've ever been to is Sri Pra Phai in Woodside, Queens. Actually authentic Thai food with a larger menu than street places in the country itself and the cleanliness of a New York kitchen. In Thailand, I heard a story about a restaurant that once served a prince being closed when someone was caught pissing in the kitchen.

I sat in quiet comfort listening to the sweet, delicate French that eased between them in the cool, night air. I felt like I could understand the basics of the conversation, but I had trouble thinking of anything to say. There didn't seem to be anything quite so important beyond how the restaurant had a campy, rustic mystique that I thought I might have seen before.

"Jake, why don't you join in?" Maeva asked.

"I just like to listen," I said.

"We'd like to hear you practice some French," she responded and smiled.

"Hmm, *bien, pour quoi? Mon Français n'est pas l'meilleur. Mais, parce que le joli femme dit, je voudrais dire, le nuit est... est, the, j'adore le nuit et le* Bangkok," I said. They laughed, and we toasted in a rowdy «cheers» to Bangkok.

I took a long drink of Chang and watched as they resumed conversation. I interjected a few times, and the owner came out and chatted to us in English. He had been in America some years before and liked to watch European soccer.

He motioned to a TV by the bar playing a match from the Premier League. He stayed awhile because the French girls traded jokes with him.

The night took its time, and I watched a few more Thai locals filter in, but we were gone before most of the crowd came.

• • •

Sun poured in from the balcony where my wide, glass sliding doors stood open. It flowed in with thick heat drawing out beads of sweat along my pale, bare thighs and casting a golden hue on every inch of the room despite my balcony facing near dead south.

Maeva knocked on the door. At least I assumed it was her because we shared a bathroom. I pulled myself to the edge of the plus-size single bed to find my phone and check the time. Not even 8 a.m. What did she want?

My iPhone would become my computer as my laptop handled the heat with the same innate inability that a hand handles shark teeth. It would practically all but melt apart within those four months.

The wind grew steadily, licking my slick skin. Maeva called again from the door.

"*Un minut, s'il vous plait,*" I said. I thought to myself that I shouldn't have been so formal. I sounded too abrupt. I threw on some clothes. A pair of jeans and a moist T-shirt.

"Jake," she said nervously at the door. We had still only met the weekend before.

"Yes? If you'd like the shower first, please take it."

"I already showered."

"Then, what is it that you need?" I felt like I should smirk as I said the words, but I didn't. I felt inwardly triumphant as this beautiful French girl stood in little more than a towel with her hair wrapped talking to me about who was to shower first.

"Jake, when you use the toilet, could you please clean it afterwards?" She blushed, clearly embarrassed by her question. I was, too, but I nodded. She continued, "I cleaned it this morning, but in the future…" I nodded again and closed the door slowly. From then on, I would clean that thing immediately after every use.

"Are you all right?" she called after me.

"*Oui,*" I said. "I'll take a shower in ten."

"Minutes?"

"Yes."

"Do you still want to go to the school together?"

"Sure thing." I came out of the room wrapped in only a towel.

"Oh," she said and looked surprised. I had been lifting heavily at the time, so she got to see me at my best.

"Going into the shower now. I'll just be a second."

"We want to take the 9:00 a.m. shuttle," she said as she walked to the kitchen.

"Okay," I replied and went into the bathroom.

There are a lot of things that can be said about a foreign country's bathrooms. I mean, seriously. That is one of the small joys of traveling that I hope everyone gets an opportunity to experience.

Whether it's hovering over a dugout, using an Asian-style toilet in a Tokyo subway station and realizing there is no toilet paper, or finding yourself in a co-ed restroom in Italy, you really have to take the latrines as they come.

Attached to the right of each Thai toilet was this nifty little tool that shot out a soft (ideally) burst of water. A friend of mine, L, who'd later become one of my best friends in Thailand, affectionately coined the term "Bum Gun" for them. There was also a detachable shower head which made cleaning up your entire bathroom easy.

I took my soap from the wall and washed up in a cold shower. The heat and humidity of Bangkok offset the temperature of the water, and I could see my skin glow in the humidity as I shaved in the mirror. Clogged pores were suddenly no longer a problem.

I joined the French group for the 9 a.m. shuttle, and it pulled out from Nonsi's side gate with a chug. The girls chatted, and I watched the road as we eased down the small soi and out toward Chua Phloeng. I admired the girls' conversational style as the van pulled onto Chua only to be stuck in traffic.

There was something instinctual and pure about being French that I couldn't hold onto completely any longer than it took me to wonder at their general frankness. They simply had no care to filter their tone, and in this case, even though I didn't understand a word that they were saying, I understood that they were not happy with the traffic.

We sat for nearly half an hour at an intersection just south of Rama IV as motorbikes weaved between us. From there, the journey felt a lot faster, but when we finally came to a halt in the middle of the Chulalongkorn campus, a normally ten-minute drive had taken us closer to fifty minutes. One of many remarkable feats to be achieved on the Bangkok roads.

When I squeezed out of the air conditioning after them into the humidity of a Bangkok January, it finally hit me that I had really made it here. While I certainly thought that I had worked hard as a student, the potential of studying abroad for a semester had seemed as fanciful as Alice's trip to Wonderland.

And yet, here I stood on another country's most famous college campus, surrounded by French ladies, headed to meet Thai buddies who would show us around Chamchuri Square, MBK, and Siam Paragon on a tour of the campus and surrounding area.

The highly improbable had already become reality, and the trip hadn't even really begun. We had so many more first Thailand experiences to come.

We had a busy day planned, but while I had playfully warned the girls that there were a lot of shopping malls in Bangkok, having been there briefly before, I, too, was quickly at a loss for words. Until we had gone to three different malls just to get the stuff we needed for daily life as international students, including phones and debit cards, it hadn't truly set in how much shopping would define our time in Bangkok.

There were three major shopping centers around Chula, each important in their own right and all with almost a completely different set of shops and restaurants. In a way these make up the central shopping center of Bangkok, but also each shopping center littered throughout the city had an entirely different vibe.

The first, and the one that we frequented the most, was Chamchuri Square. This was just south of the BBA building and housed one of the MRT stations. Wonderful. It also had six different coffee shops. One of which was Starbucks, so of course, we went there often. My second choice was True Coffee—maybe because it had better wi-fi (that was also free) and cuter baristas?

Chamchuri Square also had the bookstore, the photo booth where we took the photos for our IDs, and the bank where I got my local ATM card.

The next shopping center we went to was MBK. You couldn't find a more interesting mall. In some ways it helped that the indoor maze felt like something sleazy had been pumped in through the ventilation system. We were constantly haggling from floor to floor. There were kiosks between the more standard store fronts set up along the sides.

At first, the layout of the vendors didn't appear to have any rhyme or reason, but the chaos was more controlled than I initially realized. That's one of the things that made it such an experience. That and the fact that four shops within eyeshot would be selling the same products at vastly different prices.

There were also serious bespoke suit stores that would be my first real taste of one of Bangkok's premier industries. Those places were cheap, so the prices after bargaining could actually be quite favorable. However, there are many more places to get suits made in Bangkok.

Additionally, there was a bowling alley and a gaming room on the top floor, a set of restaurants just below that, and a massive hall of electronics shops where we'd bargain for a halfway decent smart phone that I wouldn't mind losing if I got too blind drunk.

Thankfully, I never lost it. More thankfully, I got blind drunk plenty.

A lot of them had grocery stores in the basement, including the *piece du resistance*. The *crème de la crème*. Siam Paragon, one of the largest malls in Thailand. It took all the things other shopping malls had and made them ten times better, cleaner, fancier, and cooler.

On that first day, we went to the MBK basement, found some food that reminded us of home and cabbed back from the taxi stand together.

The loose band broke up pretty quickly. Maybe because of the language barrier, but also because I made a good friend. Later, when we would go to the school together for an official tour of the grounds, I would meet the Germans.

chapter two

The Germans

The elevator doors slid open to a wave of humidity, and I stepped out in my old, black loafers and my new school uniform. I played with the sunglasses at my chest and went for the door to the lobby.

My heart jumped. The girl in white. I saw her open the glass entry doors to the lobby as I came out of the elevator.

Her hands looked small and soft. Her smooth skin caught the morning sun as her official uniform, a blue pleated skirt, shook in the wind from the front door revealing a paler portion of her bare thigh.

She had buttoned the white shirt of her school uniform tight, revealing her ample chest. I went out the door, running my hand through my hair, and made it through the lobby in what felt like three strides.

I heard the engine. I saw the shuttle door close. The van lurched up the slope of the driveway and toward the way it had gone the other day when the French girls and I had sat through the morning traffic.

I had missed the girl in white again.

I put my sunglasses on and went down along the patio space with its tables, chairs, and benches set between green trees and plants. The day and the hot season were still in their beginnings, and the sun didn't beat down with the same intense heat that it would later.

I smiled to the staff at the little restaurant outside our apartment building and waved off the motorbike taxi guys who offered a fifty-baht ride to the MRT. Instead, since I was early anyway, I walked along the road down to Chua Phloeng. In later days, this walk would become so unbearably hot that I'd pay for the ride, but under the not yet blistering heat of the January sun, I could meander along the side roads in my school uniform.

On Chua Phloeng, I heard the thunderous barking of strays that had camped out in the building on the corner. While I didn't want to seem afraid, I skipped forward and looked back pulling my sunglasses down slightly so I could see more clearly.

The dogs weren't following, but I listened for their footsteps as I went along the busy road in the morning traffic.

In some places, the road was smeared with shit. I didn't know whether it was from more stray dogs or homeless people who had disappeared as the morning came.

I couldn't see the shanties along the tracks from this vantage point, but the sidewalk snaked along the road opposite the rusted and forgotten car graveyard that was caged in beneath the highway. Just past this, the sidewalk ran out, and I ducked between some cars watching for bikers as I went along a stretch of the road beneath the highway that had a fenced-off pedestrian "walkway" sandwiched between the traffic speeding in either direction.

I may have passed the shuttle at one point given the rate of traffic. Eventually, I stepped over the rusted fence, one of those bumper-like guard rails, and a space of parked motorbikes along the side of the road at the main intersection. This is where the cops would stand if they were directing or watching traffic.

I passed over the tracks and walked along Rama IV to the MRT station where a smaller set of motorbike taxi drivers in different colored uniforms chatted and chewed at the entrance. Only customers and ladies in high heels seemed to shake them from their forlorn stares at the lines of cars.

The MRT station was clean and cold. I stood under the fans of the air conditioner and waited for the train to come. I rode it a stop or two to Chamchuri Square. I came out underneath Tesco and then got to the level of Starbucks, which the French ladies had snubbed the other day.

The air was good and cold, but I had to exit the back doors into the humidity again, which forced beads of sweat to run down the edges of my hair and neck. I watched a Mercedes pass by before crossing the street onto the Chulalongkorn grounds.

The BBA tower, where most of our classes would be, was on the right, and the administration offices as well as some other classes were in a two-story, more traditional looking building on the left.

This morning, I headed into the smaller building as I was meeting a group for a tour of either the campus or the BBA facilities. To be honest, I can't really remember much of the tour. The main thing I remember from that day was the trio of Germans I met.

Finnias, Victor, and Clarissa.

The program director showed us around and introduced us to a few of the Thai girls who were our classmates. This particularly cute one was interested in Finnias, and when we were introducing ourselves, we realized that we all lived at Nonsi. They must have been on the shuttle with the girl in white, I thought to myself.

The clearest picture from that moment was Finnias. He introduced himself in an American accent like he came from the

Midwest, so smoothly that I mistook him for American at first. But he also had a style that appeared to be copied from a surfer magazine. He was both so serious and calm that being around him was easy. Finnias was nicknamed Finn, and every time he would introduce himself it would be as such. "My name is Finnias, but you can call me Finn. Like a dolphin's fin," he would say, and he would put his hand in the shape of a fin above his forehead and salsa in place with a wink.

Trying to remember where it exactly started is a little difficult, but it might be important to note that I was in one of my more intense periods of diet and exercise before coming on the trip. So was Finn. He clearly looked like he worked out, and at some point on the tour one of us must have asked.

"Hey, where is the gym? I heard there was a pretty big one somewhere on campus."

"Here, let me show you guys."

"Dude, do you lift, too? I've been planning to find a buddy to go lifting with."

"Yeah, I'm down. Let's do it."

"We can swap exercise routines."

"Sounds sick, let's do it."

And so, a gym partnership was born, and for the majority of our time in Bangkok, it was just about the best time that I spent with anyone.

Needless to say, we immediately became best friends, and until it all got fucked up later, we were inseparable.

• • •

The sun grew hotter, and the air hung heavy with a thin fog of humidity. I always felt like I could cut the air with a butter knife, but I could never see this hidden veil—a transparent half-poison, half-moisturizer that stuck to your skin. It took some getting used to.

I ran along the track outside the gym with determination. My sweat ran thick, and my breath choked on the watery air like stumbling into a damp, wet cloud on a high mountain where the oxygen is thin. But we were so close to the ground that I had a hard time figuring out why it was so difficult to breathe.

The open-air track was on the fourth floor and looked out over much of the campus. The business school was blocked by the elevators on the southeast side, but I had a good view of the northeast half of campus stretched out toward the BTS which must have been hidden like a vale between the school and the Siam shopping malls.

I finished off my water bottle and filled it again under a cooler at the south end of the track and went back up to the gym to sit in the air conditioning as Finn finished his extra sets. We had lifted for a good amount of time, and then I had gone out into the heat to do some aerobics while he had gone for another few sets on the chest equipment.

Bangkok was a world of contrasts, and the Chulalongkorn gym was no different. Like any gym, it had plenty of people who didn't know what they were doing. However, for the most part, there were very few guys and those who were there seemed to skip the most effective weight machines.

We did meet one really fit guy that had a hell of a sturdy-looking body packed into something like a 150-pound frame. Probably could be a nasty welterweight, but I was going on 200 pounds, and at the time, I lost weight if I didn't scarf down beef and rice every night after we went lifting.

I sat there watching and wondering at the girls trying to get in shape, hoping that they wouldn't give up and that someday they would achieve some measure of happiness even if it took a few grueling days a week plugging away at the treadmills while they wore full makeup.

One of the strange treats were the dance groups that would sometimes take up the CrossFit area full of mirrors, medicine balls, and yoga mats. Sometimes as I'd run around the track, I'd see them practicing different dance routines. Perhaps the same routines that I'd later see at the annual Chulalongkorn-Thammasat soccer match that had been held for sixty-eight years straight.

Of course, I never lingered long, but I always felt an extra boost of motivation as I rounded the corner, knowing they were there. Maybe they were watching. Likely not, but I had been told I was a decent-looking fellow, and it couldn't hurt to hope.

I never hung my hat too high on the hopes of finding a Thai woman, especially with the girl in white on my mind, but I wasn't shy about any pursuit of women especially in the first days that we explored Bangkok.

"What do you want to do tonight?" Finn asked as I pushed forward on a chest press machine.

"Don't know. Got any ideas?"

"Do you like to smoke hookah?" he asked.

"Yeah," I said. I used to go to this place in Milwaukee with a friend of mine called Casablanca. "Do you want to look for a place here?"

"Really? Is it popular in the states?" he asked, having picked up a little bit of lingo from me already.

"Not sure. It's getting popular," I said. "I think Milwaukee is kind of a diverse town. A lot of students from the Middle East."

"It's getting a lot more popular in Germany. I'll have to show you one of my favorite rap songs."

"So, hookah tonight?"

"Maybe. I'll have to see if we can find a place. I'll text you later."

"Sure," I said. "Want to head back now?"

"Yeah."

We went to the locker room and showered and bagged our clothes and took the elevators down to the ground level. At his insistence, we stopped at this little shop next to the gym which served protein shakes.

They were damn good. It never took a lot of convincing to get me to do anything, even though I considered myself inherently skeptical.

We had the same style shake. Chocolate and banana with protein powder and milk. They made it in front of us in a blender with Nestlé chocolate sauce and a whole banana.

The Thai didn't fuss around with any extras like we sometimes do in the states. No pre-made mixes. They just do it right in front of you. If you ask for a fruit shake, they literally just throw fruit, ice, and sugar water into a blender. As simple as it gets, and it was so good. Dragonfruit, passionfruit, any type of fruit.

Finn flirted with the girls behind the counter, and I could see the way they stared at him. They were cute girls, but even though I've had a decent reputation for my looks, Finn outshined me wherever we went. Luckily, I didn't go with him everywhere.

Finn smiled at me. "What's wrong? Be nice." He tapped my shoulder.

"They like you, man. You're the good-looking one."

"I have a girlfriend." He chuckled. "You don't."

"True, but..."

"But, what?"

"There's this girl at Nonsi that I've been interested in."

"Really, what's her name?" he asked.

"Haven't met her yet."

"Then keep your options open." He drank from his shake and played with his sunglasses as we sat there on the white plastic furniture.

"True, yeah, I should, but I want to give it a chance first."

"It will happen or it won't. Don't force it."

"Exactly," I replied and stirred my shake.

"Let me know when you finally meet the mystery girl, okay?"

"Definitely," I replied, and we left Chulalongkorn as the sun still hung high in the midday sky.

Going to the gym, chocolate banana shakes, and suit shopping on Soi 8 became a routine for us, but it took time to make it consistent.

There were a lot of good memories to share as the days grew longer and the sun stood unmarred by the clouds of future storms. January and February had only clear skies for us, and the high temperatures weren't so bad yet that we couldn't make our way around the city during the day in dress shirts.

Our days were lazy and lost in a haze of hope and budding youth. We lusted for all things. Suits, women, money. The future lay in wait for us, so close that we could taste it. Our minds clicked in stride as we thought of the grand gestures that we could someday make.

And what is lust but that yearning for a taste of youth? Ambition and the hope that we may capture something for ourselves. In a song, in a story. With a check for the amount in the brochure. We longed to have something to share someday, but we longed even more to live in a moment beyond ourselves.

These thoughts only amount to the hope that we might prove something happened here. Even now, I look back and try to make sense of it all, to bring meaning to the whole adventure. But I wonder if there ever was any real meaning to it, and I'm lost now, chasing the figment of a past that grew too wonderful in the natural fading of time.

Or perhaps not. Perhaps I'll find it again. That feeling I had when the ladies smiled at Finn and I, and the possibilities seemed limitless.

• • •

Since we were both men of action, it took very little time for us to head out together for hookah. Finn and I shared a love of breathing in flavored steam.

The two of us embarked on a life-changing trip to the Arab district. I had been told to avoid this area and all the areas surrounding it, Soi 11 and Soi 4 included. Finn had spent a night looking up the best hookah spots and found the best one at the district's center.

I can't remember if we took a cab or experimented with the MRT, but we found ourselves, one sunny early evening, walking between the dollar pop-up shops along the bright, long, and rich road of Sukhumvit.

What little I had heard about this stretch of Sukhumvit made it sound like a ratchety place for the seedy and nefarious even though that isn't really completely true, but it's the best I can describe its reputation.

We were more astutely described as within or between or surrounded by the seedy and nefarious. At times we were within a bubble, set off from the late-night extravaganzas. Inside and outside the bubble were expensive apartments, costing seven thousand dollars a month at a time when we were paying about three hundred to live a five-minute drive down a side street. Granted, by some ironic unreality of traffic and the incapability of decades-old road planning, it took a minimum of thirty minutes to get to that same place, but to pay seven thousand dollars to live in a "nice" apartment off Sukhumvit seemed insane.

We weaved through foot traffic consisting of locals and tourists perusing hundreds of pop-up shops that stretched along the north side of Sukhumvit for miles. We headed back along the road toward the west to the direction of things like Central-World and Siam Center, which were important hubs.

We pointed out iconic symbols on cheap T-shirts and remarked on fake watches, but mostly we kept an eye on our things and joked about the repetitiveness of these places. Between the streets of Soi 11 and Soi 5, the Arab district where we would get our hookah, there must have been at least thirty shops on the side of Sukhumvit alone, and more down the sois.

As we walked, we noticed our first Thai hookers. There were three of them on the corner. You may think to yourself, they couldn't have been hookers, or wonder how we could tell, but we just could. They were hookers as clear as a Bangkok day is bright, as clear as the night is black and the winter's snow is white.

They were dressed in red G-strings and revealing bras that covered only their nipples. Their seven-inch, clear high heels, known as stripper pumps, looked painful as they stood there idly. Innocently, Finn and I smiled at each other.

These girls, smoking cigarettes idly in the sun, had tanned skin, creamy, and shaved. Even their arms glistened in the late sun. Their muscles were taut and their posture impeccable. Dark, beady eyes blinked beneath thick eyelashes draped by black eyeliner and dark mascara. One could not fail to miss the false perkiness of their size-D chests.

It stands out so forcefully in my mind due to the preposterousness of the experience. Here were these three women standing in nothing waiting for a john like me to walk up and say, "Let's fuck."

It would have been that simple, and it would have been over just as fast. And yet, their pure sexuality, wanton in its lack of any vague whimsicality, pressed into our minds a very real femininity that the likes of Kendall, Kylie, or any kind of Kardashian-Jenner clone or ilk would later try to replicate.

Every time I see a girl with overdone makeup and fake eyelashes today, I think of those three hookers. They were so nonchalant, and everyone else around them, the Thai I mean, accepted their appearance as immutable fact.

Finn and I laughed off the shock as we went up the street and took a right into the Arabic area which may have been one of the cleanest and safest (no alcohol within) parts of the city. The only odd thing was the massage parlor at the back of one of the side streets which staffed only ladyboys.

We passed the hookah bar on our first go and wound up walking past them. They excitedly called out to Finn and me, which was a technique of all those types of places, but we scampered away from them and their red underwear and plastic faces and continued down the street until we found the place that we wanted.

It was busy on the inside and the daylight was almost gone, so we took a spot out front of the shop, joining a crowd of guys that were watching Iran play Bahrain in a soccer match.

Bahrain had the better tactics, but Iran had the stronger side. I think at one point it was tied one to one. I can't remember which side the group was rooting for, but I know that there was at least one person who was as excited for his team as I was for mine. When the winning goal was scored, he ran into the street and yelled triumphantly at the top of his lungs with his fists clenched in the air.

We got the hookah and smoked as the sun went away, blowing thick wafts of white steam into the heavy and humid air. We ate lamb skewers and hummus and talked about our plans for the city and traveling in the neighboring countries. I had already been to a couple, so I shared some insights, but there was a lot of ground to cover and too many options to choose from.

Clearer now than anything was how well we got along with each other. We both wanted to get suits tailored and to exercise regularly. We stayed until the end of the game, and the guys were excited that their team had won.

We had a very good meal at a very good price and felt as good as ever as we left the district to return to the Sukhumvit main road to hail a cab back to Nonsi Residence.

It was a one-way street, and at this time of day we had to grab a cab from the other side if we wanted to take the quickest route home, so we were in for a surprise.

Every single one of those pop-up stores that sold absolute crap just a few hours before had been converted into an open-air bar. There must have been at least fifty bottles of liquor on each one. They only served the hard stuff, no beer, and in front of each one were a few chairs.

You might think that these impossible dives wouldn't expect much traffic at two in the morning, but they did. Each of these spots had at least one, and usually three or four, hookers at them.

How do I know that they were hookers? Because they grabbed my dick and told me. Yes, they grabbed both of our crotches as we passed, heading for the walkway that took us over Sukhumvit to the other side, where we would get a cab home.

It was an unreal procession as we drifted along that busy street and these girls just off work pulled at our arms and asked us if we wanted to share a hard, rough night together in a nearby hotel room. I had no intention. Finn got even more attention, but we passed by easily having had more than our egos stroked in the five minutes that it took us to clear the pop-up bars.

One of the hookers didn't look at us as we passed, and by the curve of her face, I knew immediately that she was a ladyboy. She has cut the vision of Thailand's third gender for me ever since. Her beautiful, assertive, and dominant features were imposing, but they lacked any feminine timidity. I often wonder what arousal or interest would look like in the eyes of a ladyboy besides the leer of masculine sexual excitement. Perhaps the masculine smirk replaced the feminine gaiety of the other hookers. Perhaps she had already had enough work.

Our night ended with a grand finale as we sneaked by a row of potted evergreen trees that cut off the pop-up bars. A group of hookers stood talking together, and a pretty, little thing in a tight blue dress that shimmered in the light like fish scales jumped on Finn's back and yelled, "Oh you so pretty, I fuck you for free."

As he laughed it off and told her that he had a girlfriend, we came upon a hotel with nightly rooms that stood slightly away from the road. That was a real dive. Wouldn't be surprised if the carpets were brown shag and stained in each room.

There must have been somewhere between ten and twenty hookers on the front steps. Some with cigarettes. Some still in their heels. Others twirling them on their fingers. We were at the staircase at last, took the walkway across the street, and had a cab immediately.

In five minutes, we were standing in Nonsi's lobby flushed with excitement and laughing at the absolute absurdity of the experience, promising each other that we would meet the next morning for breakfast and reflect further at one of the tables on the patio.

I took a cold shower before going to sleep and slept naked with the window open.

• • •

The next morning, I grabbed a towel, wrapped it around my waist, and took another cold shower. It was the best I could do to beat the heat, but there was really no beating it. It was a fact of life.

I went downstairs and ordered an American breakfast from the Nonsi restaurant. Eggs, bacon, toast, and orange juice. I added a Thai iced coffee for fifty baht, and the total came out to be 210, which was somewhere between six and seven dollars. A Starbucks latte still cost five bucks at Chamchuri Square.

I relaxed at one of the green tables on the patio waiting for Finn and the food. I lay back against the chair with my sunglasses resting precariously on my cheeks. My flip-flops hung off my toes as my feet rested on one end of the chair. My phone sat dark and lonely on the table when something caught the corner of my eye. A slight movement, and I saw her walking up to the desk to order breakfast.

The large Thai iced coffee in front of me perspired large tears that pooled on the glass table below it. I looked out from beneath my glasses at the slender profile in a summer dress tapping at her cheek and hiding her skin under a hat while ordering breakfast from the patient little Thai girl, Cindy.

From here, she was about the size of one of those lazy little droplets of water that slipped off the side of the plastic cup, but I knew it was her. The girl in white. She came back to sit alone across from me at the next table, and I wondered if I looked like some kind of passed out junkie.

I stretched my neck and took a sip from my coffee. She smiled again, and I made my move. I picked up my wallet and phone with the other hand and sat myself opposite her as the early morning granted us both a moment's respite from prying eyes and the gossip of the other tenants.

"Mind if I join you?" I asked as I sat.

"Not at all."

We sat there in silence staring into each other's eyes. I mirrored her posture, and I said, "My name's Jake. Are you American?"

"Mischa," she replied. "Yes."

"Thought so." We both smiled. I took a sip of my drink.

"What are you up to in Bangkok?"

"I'm a student at Chulalongkorn," I said. "You?"

"I am, too. Though I wouldn't mind giving it up to be one of those models running around here."

"You could be one of them, but why? Most of them want to be university students."

"How do you know?"

"I've asked them."

My breakfast was brought out.

I said thank you in Thai, and Mischa and I had a brief moment of arguing who had ordered the American breakfast first before we both gave into the other.

"Where are you from?" I asked.

"Seattle area."

"Cool. I'm from Madison."

She shifted, seemingly uncomfortable.

Finn appeared and said, "Man, what a night."

"Yeah," I said.

"Did you order?" he asked and looked to Mischa.

I nodded.

"I'll be right back." He smiled and went to chat and flirt with Cindy.

"I'll let you two eat alone," Mischa said, and she moved a few tables away with her food.

"That was her, wasn't it?" Finn whispered a little too loudly as he came back. I made a face at him to shut it, but he didn't quite take the hint.

I changed the subject. "How'd you sleep?" I asked him.

"Like a baby." Finn mimed the words as he sat down and put on a pair of aviator sunglasses. While my sunglasses made me look like something out of a *Terminator* movie, Finn looked like he was trying out for a Tom Cruise biopic. The cut of his shirt showed off his biceps, and he smiled. He was a good-looking guy, and the look fit him.

Cindy smiled as she came out to deliver my food.

"What a night," Finn repeated. He smiled at Cindy, too, as we exchanged again in Thai. "Eat, man. You're getting pretty good at speaking Thai."

"Thanks," I said. "Nowhere as good as you, though." He could order in Thai. I just had decent pronunciation of a few words. I started organizing my food into egg sandwiches between a few final sips from the tall and sweet and cold Thai coffee.

"Still want to head to the gym later?" he asked.

"Yeah," I said.

"Any other plans?"

"None yet. What are you thinking?"

"One of the guys was telling me about Soi Cowboy. I was thinking of inviting a few people to go and heading over there tonight. Have you been?"

Everyone liked to ask me if I had been to a place, and I most often had to say no.

"Not yet." I took a bite of my sandwich. "But, I have heard of it. When were you thinking of heading over there?"

"I don't know. Ten, eleven."

"Sounds good," I replied and finished the sandwich. Finn's food came, and we ate for a little bit as friends came out and went off to their own plans with smiles and hellos.

"Did you want to go suit shopping soon?" I asked.

"Yeah, I was thinking tomorrow after class. What do you think? We'll be out around four and can take the BTS to those places I looked up."

"Which places?"

"The ones I sent you the other day."

"Oh, yeah. Tim's Fashion? And umm…"

"The Tailor on Eight."

"Yeah, that's it," I said. "I still think the first step to any shopping experience is getting some exposure to what's out there. I say that we take some time over at Siam Paragon to go through some of the places like Hugo Boss and Armani."

"They're expensive."

"No shit."

"They won't let us try anything on."

"They probably will, but it really doesn't matter. It's just to get an idea of what's available. For example, I still can't figure out what makes a Zegna suit worth twenty-five hundred dollars, but I've been too chickenshit to walk in and ask. No better place in the world to figure it out."

He held up a hand. "Who is that, by the way? Is she your mystery girl?" I followed his eyes and waited for them to hit the glass doors before looking back to make sure he was still talking about Mischa and to take a second look.

"Yes. That right there is easily the most beautiful woman that I have ever seen," I said.

"What's her name?"

"Mischa."

"Did you get her number?"

"You came in and interrupted it." When I checked back, I could see that she was flipping through a travel guide and coming closer to the glass window of the lobby. As she neared, the sun momentarily darkened, and we could see each other easily through the glass.

At that moment, as fate would have it, she looked out the window. Our eyes met again. She looked down and smiled and then looked up with the grin still painted on her lips just the way she had that first night I saw her.

Someone called her, and she looked away and then she was gone.

"Man, you got to talk to her again," Finn said.

"I will."

"You should go now."

"I'll talk to her. She's a student at Chula, too. I'll see her sometime."

"I can't believe how calm you are about this right now. That girl is too pretty to let go."

"I know," I said and finished my breakfast. "Do you want to meet down here in twenty minutes to head to the gym?"

When I went inside and up the elevators, Mischa was long gone. I got my stuff ready to head to Chula with Finn for one of our lifting sessions.

I couldn't help but think that it was a modern world and a modern dating scene. Maybe she'd ask me out, but I couldn't pester or chase her. Both of those things were so *passé*. Of course, in reality, she wouldn't come to me. But, I still had to let it happen naturally.

Maybe we'd end up in the Nonsi gym at the same time, and I'd say something like, "Hi, I know we met over breakfast the other day. You're that super, uber beautiful girl from Seattle that I've seen running around in that little pleated skirt, right? Mischa? Wanna meet at the pool later?"

Maybe it would work and we'd hit it off, or maybe I'd slip on a word or say something stupid, and my deepest fear of losing that moment with a beautiful woman from back home would be lost forever.

• • •

Hung out in the garden of plenty that Bangkok became stood a short street off a busy road that swarmed with cabs like gnats to the sweet smell of warm peaches baking in the harsh sun—Soi Cowboy.

Before it, after it. I honestly never really cared much for anything beyond finding someone single that would share some time with me, but everyone always pressed upon me the thought that I wanted something else.

It must have been this perceived innocence that shares a bed with smooth skin. If I ever did want or need or desire to chase the night away with the flowers of timid youth, Soi Cowboy satisfied that passion for lusts unconquered and then some.

The first time I went was with the Germans. Clarissa, Finn, and Victor. There might have been another girl there, too. I honestly can't remember. I got a little drunk and a little flustered.

It started the same as the night we left the Arab district where the ladies from the pop-up bars had tenderly chased us along the curve of the long road of Sukhumvit.

To talk about Soi Cowboy is like reciting some crooked male fantasy out of a guidebook for sin. There were about twelve bars spread evenly on each side of the road. But honestly, there were only three that mattered.

The blue one on the left had the simplest name that I can't remember anymore. We'll call it Lotus. There was also the red one in the middle, Suzie Wong's, and on the other side, Bacarra, which was larger still and also red.

By the time I left Bangkok, I had been to all twelve bars at some point or another, but those three were the ones that we would go to more than once. Certainly no other place in the world legitimized paid sex so forcefully.

Each bar had at least four good-looking girls in G-strings and pumps shaking their asses out in front of their respective bars. Sometimes these girls worked both the door and the inside, but usually they were just there to pull at your tender parts and whisper into your ear to get you to come inside.

One girl playfully bit my stomach just above my pant line. Yes, she was a girl. The ladyboys had their own spot and generally weren't as aggressive unless you showed interest. In each of these regions of the city, there was at least one ladyboy go-go bar. And they usually were the tallest, fittest, prettiest of all the bars.

That night, we made it down the length of the street and went to Baccara. Finn had heard it was the best one, so we made it our first stop despite the aggressive pleas of the door girls along the way. It certainly earned whatever reputation it had.

We all handled ourselves pretty well in Baccara, which I must say is the most surprising thing about the experience. We went in on the main floor, and there were at least fifteen girls dancing in school-girl uniforms on an elevated stage in frosted glass heels and knee-high socks.

They were surrounded by stadium seating full of Asian men in suits. There was a large window above the girls that matched their shoes opening on another set of less attractive girls in the same outfits but without panties.

According to Finn, even if there were seats downstairs, we wanted the bar on the second floor. We went along the front of the crowd to the back-right corner where a thin staircase took us up to the girls on the second floor.

Some looked more confident than others. Some looked out of place or shy. Since that first moment in BKK, I've learned that some cultures order one attitude over the other.

We now had a better view of the floor, and I noticed for the first time that each girl had a red pin attached to her skirt. It looked like a cross between a poker chip and a senate campaign pin and each pin had a yellow number on it.

If you were interested in a girl, you had to call the *Mamasan*, but at most of the other places, it was one-on-one negotiation.

We went to the bar and each grabbed a drink. When the song stopped, the girls took off their bras and shook their tits. There seems to be a misconception that Asians aren't well endowed, but that's not true.

In addition to the schoolgirls, there were smoking hot Thai women in black dresses, leggings, and stilettos who came around. One grabbed my crotch and winked. Naturally, I wanted to stay, but we were finished at Baccara, and we drifted back down the street until we hit Lotus.

Lotus was a little more proper of a place and had much prettier, and most importantly, adult women. This, I learned, is because some of them were only paid dancers. Quite shocking. Coyote girls, they were called, and they weren't subject to the same strict rules as the other dancers.

But when we came in, this cute little thing, just shorter than me in heels with legs like a doe, saddled up to me and whispered into my ear for a drink. I shook my head and smiled. This was back when the girls still called me innocent, but she wasn't about to be deterred.

She played this naïve act like a new girl to the city, and everyone gave me a hard time afterward for wanting to "save" her. But you must realize I was never as tender-hearted as people seemed to think. I was too cheap to buy a pretty girl a drink. What was I going to do to help her? Nothing.

About the only thing I had was a meaningless moral line in the sand to not sleep with a hooker. A promise I made sure to keep myself from breaking. When I went on a bender I didn't carry cash to the go-go bar.

After I gave my final no to her, she went up on stage in her little plaid skirt and pumps and danced with her panties right in front of my face for two songs. She didn't quite shake it like Nicki Minaj in her video for "Anaconda," but close enough.

She shook left and right like she was rubbing a towel across her butt. Only it kept her soft, pink flesh just hidden out of view until she intentionally bent forward to the song.

When she came off the stage, I finally bought her a drink and she took a real long time drinking it while she whispered into my ear that she wanted me to do dirty things to her. She "accidentally" let her hand graze against my lap, and we both knew that I wanted her badly.

When I read a book about the memoirs of a Thai girl who used to work as a hooker in Bangkok, I learned that this behavior I had experienced was basically unheard of, and she probably had actually liked me. I know, strange, but I didn't believe it then. Of course, I could have also been an easy mark.

So thankfully or not so thankfully, when we paid for our drinks and left, all I got out of that night was the group joking that she had stolen my heart. Maybe she did. She certainly acted like an innocent girl.

There is not a street in the world that has changed my personality as much as that street has. For the better, hopefully.

There are certainly streets that are just as memorable, but the stunningly grotesque world of Pussy For Sale drains on one pretty quickly, especially when it all just seems so pointless. We all know a lot of guys like to brag about how many girls they've fucked. If it's as empty as one night at Soi Cowboy, I'll pass.

• • •

The question was, did I deserve anything at all out of life? By breaking beyond some thin film of morality into a world of clear, visceral intention, was I somehow no longer someone who could be loved?

I asked myself this when I thought of the good girls at Nonsi, like Mischa. Were they too innocent and pure for a man like me who had once again glanced across the surface of the obscene in the dark night?

We all wanted to believe that we belonged somewhere in the world, and we yearned to find our place someday. But we had already lost it before we recognized it had been thrust upon us at all.

What separated us? What bound us? Bangkok stripped it bare. It left our inner "selves" naked and emotions raw. We could only ever hope to find that feeling again.

It will forever be the same. Behind us as soon as we've touched it in our mind's eye. It could only be that way. Just a fleeting glimpse of what could no longer be that held our gaze in a mere moment of triumph over the vast array of infinity that clouds out the hope that anything more than memory and emotion will stand still over time.

I wonder if, in the end, we will beg them to destroy us because we don't have any true reason to do it ourselves. In contemplating that notion and how our bonds and relationships fit into the grander scheme, I was so fatefully drawn to a true lotus caught in her own existential turmoil.

Mischa's tears hit a set of couches on a second-floor lounge area near the community washer and dryer. We had to take that route to go from my tower to the pool. I was on my way to bask in the sun and share pineapple shakes with a friend of mine from Australia when I saw her again.

Mischa held her face in her hands, and at the sound of my footsteps, she looked up. She smiled and seemed to give a shrug of her shoulders, communicating that of all the people to have happened upon her, of course it was me.

I didn't really know how she felt about me, but that shrug could have meant anything. I certainly didn't feel like I deserved any sort of kindness.

"Are you all right?" I asked.

"Not really," she said.

"Hmm, I guess I should have asked something less obvious."

"You could have."

"Is there anything that I can do to help?"

"It's all right. It's my fault for being such a mess."

"What happened? Something at home?"

"My boyfriend," she said and didn't explain much further.

"Mischa," I said as I slowly reached a hand to pat her on the shoulder, "if you need anything, let me know. I'll do what I can for you."

She wiped her eyes again and nodded. "Thank you."

We parted ways after I wished her the best, and I went up to the pool.

Defeat hung in the air like a tepid flush. She had a boyfriend, and I had felt so hopelessly romantic.

The hopes that I had slowly built up on Mischa had been snagged out from beneath me with such a simple pair of words. But she was just one girl, and I had barely known her. Other girls would certainly come to crush or build my heart, but for that moment Mischa fell from my mind. The cordiality of the group by the pool returned me to the bright, hot world of hope that was Bangkok.

I did wonder though, if I didn't have such clear scruples, could I ever lure one person away from another? I could never be anything more than monogamous myself, so I never wanted to do that to someone else.

That moment changed things between us. She recognized me as we passed, and one day as I sat enjoying that American breakfast alone in the early morning, she joined me again. A friendship was born.

• • •

"So, you finally talked to the mystery girl again?" Finn asked.

"Who?"

"The girl from breakfast the other day. The one standing in the lobby."

"Ah." I shrugged. "I did."

"And?"

"What?"

"What's her name? Where's she from?"

"Mischa. I thought I told you before," I said and continued looking through the suit fabrics one by one. I watched as tiny insects that looked like the love child of flies and moths attempted to camouflage themselves on the blues and blacks. I killed one.

"Mischa. I like that," Finn said and played with the sunglasses that hung at his chest.

"She's half-Russian, half-Japanese. Well, born in the states and still goes to school there, but yeah."

"Kinky," he said and went over to a red fabric that looked well suited for a trench coat. "You get her number this time?"

"Yeah, I did. And her Facebook."

"You're a gigolo, man."

"What?" I laughed, not sure if he knew that most Americans thought that a gigolo was a male prostitute.

"You can get any girl you like," he said. "We call you a gigolo in Germany."

"I try," I said with a wink.

"No joke, she's a real tough one. Everyone at Nonsi thinks she's the most beautiful girl there."

I grinned and looked down. "Yeah, I like her, but she's got a boyfriend."

"So, what?"

"We're friends." I shrugged.

He turned back to the displays. "What do you think of this fabric?"

"I still want to see if they have any higher end suits." I stopped the store employee as he walked by. "Hi, Tim, do you happen to have any Super 150s? The highest I see on display are 130s."

"We have a special collection of 150s. Reserved for our top clients. I wear only 150s myself," Tim said.

"Can we see those?"

He looked at us both a little funny.

"Are they Barberis, by chance?" I asked.

Finally, he nodded and said, "Yes, in fact they are."

"How much are they?"

"Twenty thousand baht for a three-piece suit, but for you, we could make an exception. If you were to actually buy something this time." He eyed me closely and smiled at Finn.

"We'd have to see something we like. I know that my friend here wants a suit or two."

Finn nodded. Tim looked at him and made a comment that he might want to come in another time when I wasn't there. I assumed he had come to think of me as more of a nuisance than the moths eating his fabrics.

"Can we see the fabrics?" I asked again.

Tim agreed but looked hesitant about it. He took out a book from a special drawer and placed it on his desk.

"These are all our finest fabrics. Super 150s, Merino wool."

The fabric samples were set out in little squares and had a little info card in the corner. They had very brief descriptions. I skipped through them and found the ones that I wanted. Blue and gray plaid. The "Prince of Wales" pattern. Damn, I really wanted those.

"How much for a two-piece in one of these?" I asked. This was probably the sixth or seventh time that we had been in this store. We had scheduled a time to have shirts tailored at another store down the street, but we hadn't decided on where to get our suits done.

"Fifteen thousand baht for you, and then I am going to have to ask you to leave and stop coming here unless you come in to purchase. If you ask any more questions, I'll think you are opening a shop of your own."

I chuckled. "Well, there you have it, Finn. These are the best. The top of the line."

"I still suggest that you get three suits and set yourself up with a substantial wardrobe," Tim said.

"Up to you, Finn," I said. "My work here seems to be done."

Tim smiled and motioned for me to exit the shop.

Finn looked over at the trench coat fabric. "Could you swap one of the suits for a trench coat?"

Tim nodded. "Sure, we can."

"And keep it the same price."

Tim mulled it over. "Okay, I can do that."

"Is the fabric waterproof?" I asked.

"We can make it waterproof," he said and motioned again to the door.

"Is that an additional charge?" I asked.

Tim shook his head.

Finn took out his phone and showed a picture of a trench coat with an oversized popped collar. "Can you make it look like this?"

Tim nodded.

"How long does the waterproofing last?" I asked.

"At least six years."

"Sounds like a good deal to me," Finn said.

I shrugged. "I'd still get the nicer suit. You could get three suits at a discount store for less, but you won't get another chance to get such a good suit at this price."

"It is not your decision," Tim said. "And now, I've allowed additional questions, please leave."

"Sure. Finn, I'll be waiting outside."

Finn left a little while later.

"What did you decide?" I asked.

"I went with the two suits and a trench coat."

"It's a good deal," I said. "Nice choice. I'll come back with you when you try it on. I'm sure he'll let me in for that."

Finn chuckled. "Let's head back to Nonsi. I'm getting kind of hungry."

"You are always hungry." We walked down the street to the end, passed the lollipop girls, and hailed a cab which took us down almost to Siam Paragon before taking the left home.

"Do you want to go see *The Hobbit* again tonight at Siam Paragon?"

"Would love to," I said.

I look back now at the Germans and think of them as direct, honest, and well-groomed. In many ways, they were similar to the Australians, who were by far the most fun.

chapter three

The Australians

I had wanted my grand gesture of love to Mischa to rank among the greatest of all time. For it to rank in the place of the legendary loves of the past. You would hear the story of that Spring of '13 around the world by hushed whisper like a secret told in the twilight of a happy evening. Serenity. Did you happen to hear the story of that American in Bangkok? Which? The one who chased the girl of his dreams and won her heart? Yes, like something out of a fairy tale.

However, now that we were relegated to friends, the Bangkok night grew into an extraordinary world more mythical than any I would ever know.

Luckily, I made a good friend, L the Australian, at Nonsi, who would guide me through the complicated network of Bangkok's nights. These distractions appeared in the winding, starlit streets with a simple celerity akin to weeds in a field of roses.

L had picked from this field before, and with a singular purpose he deigned to throw himself once again at the liminal passion of the women who swayed in the heat of the unending night.

Without any possibility of a romance with Mischa, I was no longer tethered to my own standards of action. I had no reason to walk along that meaningless line of virtue in a world wrought with sins far worse than my own. I joined L on a quest to quench that ordinary thirst which dries too quick to whet.

What did I long for but my own moments of unbroken passion? Not love, but lust as I knew lust to be where a glance becomes a dance, and the hands of an unknown lover glide against your skin in unchecked ecstasy.

Each bottle of Chang. Each glass of Johnnie Walker, and I woke to this hunt for which gentleman check their coats at the door. The eyes dilate and turn hungry. My hands, deftly simple, stroked shivering streaks against the skin of each dancer longing for impurity.

I found it. In more ways than one, but it was never intended to be so tangential. With each glancing chance at contact with the female form, I learned what changed the shade of a heart.

Even with the desire for something tangible, we all knew that what we found in those midnight meetings would spoil in the daylight when the heart longed for more than the swift thrust of one's lover.

My good intentions never stood a chance. My sense of self was nothing more than a faceless name on a page. In fact, I'd gain more respect if I was nothing but that name. For the true plight of the rose is that it has no dream of its own. It's cursed to live its life with no opinion of itself.

I wonder now whether that was the last time I would feel like I had any choice or if I lost any chance of following my heart to one destination forever. Or maybe I never really had any chance. Maybe I was always destined to be put into the box that someone else designed for me. Destined only to fit in as a relic, a memory on someone else's shelf.

Any effort to break from the tragic circumstances that we are given would be met with stiff resistance. Funny to think that

I had been raised to think that a true American was one who stepped outside the realm of boxes and norms.

But then again, that is what I was: an American in Bangkok. But also a "man" and that identity was stronger because it was a role I fit naturally. Traversing from one street after another of blaring music and colored lights casting pretty faces and tight dresses in shades of blue. Casting aside the old thoughts of finding myself a girl in the college dorms who was an eager dreamer.

This was real life. This was all that people wanted of me. To strike away the search for purpose or meaning. To leave out all the pieces of what I wanted for myself so that people could imagine my future for me.

Mischa would say that her boyfriend didn't yet think that he had become a man. At the time, I had paid my own rent and made enough money to cover much of my own expenses. I had argued that I was then a man, but I recognize in the shadowy mirror of reflection that this may not be enough. The meaning of "man" is subjective.

Maybe the meaning is to be the hunter. Maybe it is to be an object of someone else's conceptual understanding. Maybe it is to be less than one thing and more than another. Regardless of whatever purpose we were destined for, Bangkok left us to our own devices to discover our fit. We watched the world unfold without prejudice and hate. We had to find our own ways together, and it brought out the best in all of us.

I met L early on in the trip while I was still occupied most days by school and hanging out with Finn. But, Finn became busy. I don't think I had a class that started before one o'clock, and after January I had only three courses to attend once a week.

In short, there was time on our hands, and we were going to spend it having fun.

• • •

We'd go around the city for a lot of reasons, but many memories are from Ratchadapisek Road. There was a mall out there, and one day I remember L came around while I was eating my American breakfast at one of the green tables out in front of the building. "Mr. Blaine, how you going? You got a minute?"

"Yeah." I drank some coffee.

"They play hockey in Wisconsin, don't they?" L sat down opposite me and put the Thai newspaper on the table.

"What's up?"

"I read in the paper that there is a tourney in Ratchadapisek. You want to go up there and check it out with me?"

"They're playing hockey in Bangkok?"

"Yeah," L said, and for a moment we stared at each other before a smile broke over my lips. "There is a rink at the mall over there in Ratchada."

"Ha," I said and ate some bacon.

"So, you want to get on up there with me?"

"Yeah, sure, why not? What's the tourney?"

"It's like the Asian World Cup or something. All the nations in the region are there."

"Let's do it."

We took a cab out to Ratchadapisek and went up to the fourth floor of the mall. It was an interesting area of town more on the "lowie" or "Bogan" end according to L, but the mall wasn't half-bad. It stood just in between a night spot, and a soapy massage parlor called the Old Amsterdam.

The air conditioning in most malls was cranked up to unbelievable levels, but it was particularly strong in this one. Unfortunately, I brought nothing thick, but at least we went in dress shirts that kept our skin covered.

We got there too early for the first game, so we went to a movie.

We stood for the anthem to the Thai king and watched our movie.

The movie was so forgettable that I only remember the advertisement for a Thai comedy about a dead girl haunting her town that played beforehand. However, the experience of going to a movie in Bangkok was outstanding. While the theater at Siam Paragon was hands down the best theater in the world, most of the Thai theaters were exceptional. Unfortunately, this one was colder than the ice rink.

Afterward, we stood out along the edge of the rink to watch the games. There were two teams that were excellent, and over the weekend they decimated their competition.

It was wicked fun. These little guys skated along at top speeds and rocked each other with crushing checks and solid puck movement.

Games would end at up to thirty to zero. While our weeknights and weekdays would often consist of chasing a different score, we had our share of fun, sitting at a Japanese restaurant in the food court laughing at the absurdity of hockey in Thailand. Then again, Vegas and Tampa Bay host successful teams. An ice rink was certainly one way to beat the heat.

L also loved to use interesting catchphrases.

For example, he loved to *"Bring the Hammer Down."* But after a fortune-filled trip to Sri Lanka, where his love of gambling paid off, he moved onto the best catchphrase of the trip: *"How do you like me now?"*

Each time we watched one side crush another on the ice rink we would laugh and say, "How do you like me now?"

There were more than a few "How do you like me now?" moments between the two of us. Most of these related to when we were hanging out with his Aussie friends.

One of my favorites is the story of Mason and the Mixx Club.

Mason was visiting Thailand from Australia to help a friend (who may or may not have been married) decide whether her boob job was going well. She was a short Filipino girl with a pretty face and big, sexy lips living in Hong Kong.

Mason rolled up on a motorbike painted black with red flames up the sides. He joked about getting honked at for following his girl's taxi around town rather than weaving through traffic. People must have taken him for a scared white boy, but he proved as we went on our way that he was anything but.

We went off to a few places together. To be honest, I was too drunk to remember most of them. I do remember, however, the buffet night at a place called Bourbon Street which served New Orleans Cajun. Good stuff.

Mason and L hit it off with a group of career women who were looking for a fun night out, and the two of them invited the group to what would become a familiar haunt, Mixx Club.

We arrived at Mixx Club drunk out of our minds and dressed to kill. There were two rooms. We spent most of the time in the first one with a circular dance floor just in front of the DJ.

The Thai girls liked to stand in a ring around the outside or in packs at the square tables along the wall.

I took to the dance floor while the other two talked to the ladies at a velvet table in the back corner. There was a hooker who quickly started dancing with me. I saw this woman everywhere. Levels, Mixx, my apartment building coming out of some other guy's room.

Women would proposition us just about anywhere we went, and as this happened more and more often to me, I became more interested in just enjoying my time out. Almost every time I hit the dance floor, much better dressed than most of the other men, and with the confidence to steal center stage from the few girls who would otherwise want to take it, I would attract both the ire and desire of the crowd around me.

We had recognized each other when I saw her kissing a guy goodbye at the magnetic lock door to Mischa's tower when I was eating my American breakfast one morning. She stared me down as she walked off with this grin like, "Of course he would be here."

This was the second or third time I saw her out, and I would often see her at Mixx. She was aggressive and always wore the same black dress with three slits cut out of either side. She was about my height in tall black heels and had such angry eyes that I might have thought she was standoffish.

She never actually asked me for a specific amount, but she would ask "how much to take me home." She danced close to me and looked deeply at me with the pleading eyes of a gazelle. She had an "I'm-going-to-make-you-want-me-until-you-ask-me-home" vibe. Only after rhythmically gyrating against me for fifteen minutes would she whisper in my ear to offer something to her. But I never did make an offer.

She gave an exaggerated, exasperated sigh and held up her hand before turning to walk away. She glanced back at me as she walked away with those dark eyes. Burned into memory, I never fully deciphered her intentions nor was I willing to try. But just like any memory where the intentions of another party are never fully revealed, it in some ways is "choose your own adventure." Like I said, I was willing to stand out and show up on the dance floor, and after she left, as I danced, a pair of girls in short, flowing skirts took turns grabbing and pinching me as they walked past. I pulled one close and before I knew it, this big Thai guy, about the size of a small, offensive lineman pushed me aside.

Probably six-foot-four and though woefully out of shape, he pushed somewhere between 260 and 280 pounds. He wasn't the biggest guy in the world by any means, but he was drunker than I was, and he began to box me out of the dance floor and make jokes.

"Hey little guy, why don't you show me those moves? You dance pretty good for a white guy."

I glanced over at one of the girls in a skirt. She had a light blue top and was watching me intently. Just behind her and coming around the outside of the dance floor were Mason and L, looking like they were ready to start the fight.

In somewhat of a risky move, I stole a couple of diffusion methods, picked out of the classic book *The Game.* Kristen—a Canadian girl, and one of my and L's best friends—gifted it to me, after she had finished reading it. This seemed like a rare position to have need for some of its mixed results advice.

The offensive lineman keeps joshing me and pushing me to the side, so I slapped him on the back and with a smile said, "If you want a dance off, let's dance." I did a pair of samba moves I'd picked up from a Brazilian, and he looked at me dumbfounded. Then I punched him in the shoulder and said, "Only joking."

Just joking. Speaking of catchphrases, this was a favorite Thai catchphrase, and he gave me a stupid smile and bought me a drink. On the way to the bar, after having danced with the hooker and "out-manned" the big guy, this pretty woman in a tight pink dress at the edge of the dance floor grabbed my crotch.

I told her, "One second," toasted with the big guy and joined the girl there by her lonesome as she swayed to the music.

"I thought you weren't coming back," she said.

"Pretty little thing like you, I had to."

"Buy me a drink."

"Only if you let me take you home." I winked.

"We'll see."

She gave me a smile, and as we drank together, she told me she was thirty and that she worked in the city in some field for some company that I don't care to remember. I replied in just about the most gentlemanly way I could with that much alcohol in me while telling her that I'd go down on her if she let me take her home that instant.

Sold.

I told Mason and L, who hovered nearby, that I was all good, and the girl and I took a taxi to my place while they went back to their ladies. She was tall, thin and had a pretty smile, and she told me these types of flings were a monthly habit of hers. After that night, she invited me down to Pattaya for a weekend, but I told her I had a class. Should I have gone? In retrospect, having a woman drop money on you at a lush, tropical resort near the craziest sex district in all of Thailand sounds like it would be an even better story.

But, there were more important woman who would steal my heart and maybe I wasn't willing to give up on that. Women like Mischa.

Besides, L and I, we had Bangkok.

• • •

Tyler came to Bangkok later. He traded products on the gray market and was in and out of Thailand a lot. I kid you not, L and his Aussie friends were pretty well connected and had a lot of interesting stories of their own to tell. One of their friends, Tyler, was dating one of Thailand's top supermodels. She had gotten second in some major pageant.

At her recommendation, we all went down to this place called Maggie Choo's across from Sirocco Sky Bar for its opening.

L and I got there early. The front room was a noodle bar, and the bar-bar, in its early days, was hidden behind a movable wall until you gave it a knock. We tried the noodle bar, slurping our respective bowls of noodles beneath paper lanterns and white umbrellas that were marked up in Chinese.

Two little chefs sat behind the bar looking super serious, and we got the full secretive, speakeasy treatment. We finished our noodles long before Tyler and his girl arrived, so we headed to 7-Eleven across the street while we waited.

That happened to be our lucky day. None other than the new manager of Maggie Choo's walked out of the joint. Of course, we talked to him. We bragged about it so much from then on that you'd think that we were New Yorkers.

Once we made it to Maggie Choo's, the manager ordered the staff around, and we got two rounds of drinks on the house.

Tyler and his girlfriend ordered a few bottles of wine, and invited the beautiful girl at the door, Kyra, to join us briefly. She used to bat her eyes and throw her feminine guile at me whenever I came by, but she whispered into my ear one night that at her age, she was looking for her sugar daddy.

An older man sang jazz tunes by the piano. Girls in Chinese dresses with short, black wigs lounged on swings, on top of the piano, on top of the bar, crawling around and staring from shadowy corners. Next to the entrance to the bathroom, almost completely void of light, two eyes stared back at you from the black. They followed you everywhere like eyes hidden in paintings hung in odd corners of the wall.

The place was epic. And later when the Chula kids started posting photos on Facebook, I had the self-satisfaction of remembering the smell of Kyra's perfume as her warm breath kissed my earlobes.

As we left the place, L jumped onto a tuk tuk and ordered us to hop in. He joked with the driver, who rushed over, while Tyler's girlfriend took a photo. L looked back at the camera and grinned. "How do you like me now."

• • •

People just like to assume things about others. Based on what, I don't know. Am I a good person? Are people objectively good or bad? I don't lie or cheat or steal, but I walked a strange shifting line in a foreign country. Do I get a pass on the marker of sin?

I can't imagine there is any real truth to any ultimate statement about the quality of a man that bases its conclusion on the moment, especially when the requirements for judgment are met only by unbiased observation.

But we as humans have our own worlds in which we live. We color our own narrative. We change the story. We adjust facts as they enter our minds, and all I can say is don't put that on me. If it's yours, keep it. I don't want your ideas.

I tried to live my life like a mirror, reflecting what everyone else gives. What am I, then? An echo amongst those that take on new, clearer forms of identity?

Many, I think, would have umbrage against this thought, but few, if any, will ever accept you as you are. How can we know anyone beyond ourselves? We can't capture that thought. We can't.

So, when L said to me one day that his friend Steve, who was incredibly well hung, and his Indonesian hooker girlfriend wanted to host a night of debauchery in Soi Nana, I had to say yes. I had never been.

We joined them at a street restaurant near Patpong where she worked. L refused to eat, and I should have, too. We talked and ate from this tub of raw meat, adding pieces to a pot of boiling water in the middle—similar to Korean barbecue. A dead cockroach appeared at the bottom of the pork pile.

I stopped eating. Steve and his girlfriend continued to eat. Then, we went through Patpong past the Sunrise Tacos to hail a taxi. This was the beginning of our tour, led by Steve, which would incorporate all of Soi Nana.

We came up to Soi Nana at the brisk walking pace of a man on a mission. Steve led us up to the second floor before we could even look at the girls. We went into the go-go bar on the right and sat down at center stage.

His girl bought a bunch of Ping-Pong balls that she emptied onto the stage at the girls who played with them in various ways.

A pair of the girls came over to sit on my and L's laps. My girl, dressed in silver, gave me a lap dance, smiling and laughing as she grinded against my leg, stomach and masculinity.

All for the price of one drink. We offered to pay her bar fine, so she could leave the bar for the night, but she sensed I wouldn't pay for her for the night, so she declined.

Next stop was the King's Corner. Ladyboys. Steve walked straight in there and came out with a massive group following him.

Steve was gone for only a few seconds, so I don't know what he had said or did. From the posse that followed him, this tall ladyboy with perky fake tits dropped straight to her knees in front of me. She traced her mouth over the front of my jeans and looked up at me with a smile. Her big brown eyes, wide with desire beneath sparkling eyelashes, reminded me of a demur movie star.

By the time I had turned away from her bright eyes, L and Steve were already off to the next bar. I hesitated and then chased after them. We grabbed another round and watched a pair of girls bathe each other, partially nude in a soapy bath.

And then we were off to Sunrise Tacos where we ended the night watching Steve and his girlfriend fool around on one of the couches. By this time, I felt pretty sober, and the waitress looked at me like I was the sane one.

I wasn't sure if I agreed with her.

• • •

What is life but a series of mistakes? The successes look so similar to the failures that I find myself wondering if it is merely up to perspective. Of course, we can't have it all, but we can try. And in our trying, we will certainly fail. But if failure looks like what it did back then, I would try again.

Even without Mischa at my side, I felt pretty damn good. Most days, my friends and I lounged in the pool sipping pineapple shakes.

The water was clear, blue, and cool. L was probably thinking to himself, *How do you like me now?* The sun shined nice and easy over the quiet grotto.

Finn was there, too. Though we would drift apart, he's still a painful reminder of life's transitory glimpses of good.

Once, Kristen climbed on top of a covered walkway that lined the left side of the pool and jumped in from fifteen feet.

Apart from the nights L spent nursing his liver at the Bangkok Christian, life had given us more than our fair share of happiness in such a short span of time that I felt caught up in it like everyone else. What more could we want?

It wasn't all ladyboys and Ping-Pong balls. We had good food, good friends, and all the comforts a city of sixteen million people could provide at our every beck and call. We had pool parties and vodka. Whiskey and L's unending wisdom and wit.

"Nothing good ever happens until at least 6 a.m."

Of course, you could look at it as important to wake up early. There were plenty more stories of nights out with L and his many Aussie friends at Ratchada and RCA. However, most nights ended at Sunrise Tacos on Sukhumvit after midnight, eating one of the best quesadillas I've had in my life with salsa and guac. While the foot traffic picked up into a nearby after-party night club, L and I would watch them walk past and then sometimes go in.

Perhaps the Australians would be best described for their intense gusto for life. Or you could say that they were partiers to their very core.

I guess you'd have to be an Aussie to understand the Ozzie way of life, but I hope that I came pretty close.

chapter four

The Canadians

"Jake."

Kristen sat at one of the tables at the restaurant next to the broken hole in the wall, where the chickens walked tethered between tall grass that partially hid them from view.

"Hey Kristen," I said, "that looks good. What'd you order?"

"It's called *gai krathiam*."

"That looks epic."

"Let me order one for you. The lady who works here makes it special for me. I haven't seen it anywhere else."

"How much is it?"

"Sixty baht. It's such a good deal, I was coming here even before the Nonsi restaurant closed down last week. Want to try it?"

"Yeah, for sure. I'm free." I sat down at the table across from her and motioned for her to keep eating. "How are things going? What have you been up to these last few weeks?"

"Getting around. Actually had to work on midterms. What about you?"

"Already had them."

"I'm surprised you're not with L or Finn. You never seem to be apart from those two guys. What are they doing?"

"Not sure. I've been taking it slow this morning. L found a lady friend last night, and it seems she's still with him. So, I was on my own most of last night."

"Yikes, I hate being on my own in Bangkok lately."

"Why's that?"

"A cab driver came onto me last week when I was coming home from that house party we went to."

"What did you do?"

"I pushed him off me and got out."

"Shit, I never heard of something like that happening."

"Anyways." She ate some more of her food while mine came out. "You struck out last night or what?"

"Something like that."

"Care to elaborate."

My food came, so I waited until the older, Thai woman had walked away again. "Trying to change my approach lately. Just trying to make nights fun, and not worry about finding anyone."

"Yeah, right."

"No, seriously."

"You did read that book I gave you, right?"

"Yeah." I laughed. "It actually came in use, but not in the way you'd think. Anyway, I don't mind coming home alone."

I heard the subtle whine of a pair of motorbike engines and looked back as Mischa and a girlfriend of hers passed by on a motorbike. I watched her turn the corner. She glanced back and smiled at me. I smiled back.

"You're hung up on that girl, aren't you?"

"She's left an imprint on what's left of my heart."

Kristen practically spit up her food, laughing at me.

"That's so *romantic*. Why aren't you going after her right now?"

"She's got a boyfriend."

"She noticed you. Might be something in that. If you promise not to fall in love with me, I'd love to come along with you and L on more nights out. We can taxi back here together unless I find someone to go home with."

"That's fine with me. Is there anything you're exchanging in this?"

"Sometimes you talk funny, Jake. I'll be your wingman and try to figure out what makes Mischa tick."

"Like I said, she's got a boyfriend. I may be a charlatan, but I'm a charlatan with scruples."

"Like *I* said, you talk funny, Jake. Do you know if she's still with the boyfriend?"

"No."

"I'll find out. Besides, if it doesn't work out with her, I can still be your wingman when we go out. Might help you raise your standards."

"What's that supposed to mean?"

She shook her head as if to mean, *oh nothing.* And with that partnership, my small semblance of respectability began to return to me. Kristen and I became good friends over the next few months. I had dipped down into an undercurrent of the world that had ruined many a poor boy. So what? There may be more stories where those came from, but I had come back down from whatever brink our cravings had lured us to.

Successively, over the course of the next couple months, Kristen and I ended up being pretty good for each other. Retrospectively, though, I never really paid much attention to the outcomes our relationship had at the time.

We were nothing more than friends. As wingmates, we flew together through many Bangkok nights, and she ended up keeping me out of a lot of the trouble I had been getting into.

It began on that promise that I wasn't going to fall in love with her, and I never would. Looking back, I am surprised that I didn't. She was a pretty woman with large, blue eyes.

We bonded together with L over brunch, which we had most days. Shortly after our convenient Nonsi restaurant closed in February, L tracked down an article in *The Bangkok Times* on the best brunch spots. One spot, called The Coffee Club, was an Australian chain. We went there a few times, but after having a bad experience, we sought out new places. After a couple failed attempts at finding an open place, L led us to what would be our mainstay for several months. Roast at Seenspace 13. Their menus were newspapers that showed off Australian-style roasts, but we only went there for brunch. And it was damn good.

Kristen would smoke a cigarette outside while the three of us waited, drinking from little Dixie cups of water and being stared at by slim, tall, pale Thai girls. We were the only white people there, and we lived it up.

Roast had exceptional service and saying thank you to a waiter was like petting a rescue animal. It helped that we tipped well even by American standards, and L liked to deliver his thank yous with a hand on the server's shoulder like he was delivering a catchphrase.

We'd sip on Thai iced tea. The best iced teas I've had. Right up there with a good Southern sweet tea. They weren't the milky, orange teas, which I never actually saw at a restaurant in Thailand. Though a lot of Thai people liked to make that version. These were lychee, sugar, lemon teas with the little white lychees floating in the bottom. Delicious.

I would also always ask them to make me a mocha with one of their special espressos. To be honest, I am not positive they ever followed my request even though it was on the menu. They could have just as easily told me they had used the special espresso, and I wouldn't have known the difference.

Kristen and I would start tracking down places to eat sweets in Thailand, starting with Roast. Roast had these delicious, sweet breakfasts. Like a Belgian waffle, with strawberries and powdered sugar, that you poured Valrhona chocolate over, which is literally the best chocolate in the world.

The sweets of Thailand are one of those understated secrets. That place has some truly fantastic pastry shops, like Mr. Jones' Orphanage. It's basically a restaurant version of the Island for Misfit Toys. L ended up taking us there because the guy who owned it was the same Aussie behind the excellent Maggie Choo's.

That was truly the most decadent al a mode I had ever had. It was like eating hot brownie batter in soufflé cookware that had been baked at the edges into hard cake. Then, it had the vanilla ice cream scooped into the cake soufflé.

Kristen and I went back there several times and often talked about what we wanted to find while we were in Thailand. In place of the random, morning meetings with Mischa at the Nonsi restaurant, these brunches allowed us to soak up the sun and get out to one of the nicest areas of Bangkok early in the morning.

The two of us spent a lot of time together, day and night, between the neighboring Sukhumvit sois, Thong Lor and Ekkamai.

• • •

As I sit here and think about what might or might not have been I'm drawn to one night in particular.

My world turned another way around one night with L and Kristen when we went to Escobar. Like all of our usual haunts, we couldn't stay away for long. A packed night club that catered more exclusively to upper crust young Thai and seldom, a few *farang*, it was a chill place to get stiff drinks and listen to loud music.

Seemingly every night we would say to a Thai cabbie, *"By tea Ekkah-my soy hah."* Take me to the club of my dreams.

We came to Escobar one night a little late, and the crowd was so thick that the only open pathway led to a back entrance. L led the way, lightly tapping the shoulders of guys out for a smoke as we squeezed between shoulders to try to find a way to one of the bars and a main dance floor.

The door stood, conspicuously open and without a line. As we breezed through, we had to keep moving. We had mistakenly found a back entrance to the girl's bathroom.

I could say I tried not to look, but that would be lying. There were girls passed out, standing, and more than two or three to a stall. We sped past them and out the other side. As we came out the other side, we realized that the crowd only thickened, and the bathroom had become almost an extension of the dance floor. Kristen followed just behind me, and I shot her a glance. As we walked around the bar, looking for a spot to buy a bottle, a bucket of ice, and chill, we ended up out in front of the place. L seemed to be mulling over options. There was no getting our money back for the bottle we had paid for at the door. Kristen seemed to be having fun with some of the guys waiting in line.

I wondered if it might be best to just cut our losses when this pretty girl in a light blue dress and pale heels came out with her friends and gave me a wide smile. She touched my arm. We flirted briefly, and it was fun as she thumbed my arms and seemed to purr, but then she said, "I've already dated an American. I won't do it again."

"You're already thinking about dating?"

"Hah, no, I said, I wasn't. Bye."

But as I said something back to her, she had already walked off, and I found myself alone on the street. Kristen had caught a man, and he seemed like a good guy. His friends vouched for him as I walked back from my failure to capture a girl's heart.

L had disappeared as he often did when he'd have a story for the next day, and it was just me there on the street. Kristen laughed at me. "You know, I heard this funny story the other day that I'd been planning on telling you tonight, like when we got drunk or something. I heard that girl Mischa was hung up on you, too. Maybe try giving her a call sometime. She's disappointed you haven't. Apparently, that boyfriend thing has been done for a while. Funny story, right?"

"Yeah, very funny Kristen."

"It's true, though."

"Hah, and you're telling me this now? I leave for Burma tomorrow. I'll be there for a week."

"You could say thank you. I'll put in a good word for you when I see her next."

"Thanks, Kristen."

"You know Jake, you seem to have trouble reading signals. Anyway, goodnight. Have fun in Burma if I don't see you before your flight."

"Thanks, later Kristen."

I closed the door of the taxi for her, and watched as it pulled away, leaving me alone again on the empty side street. I checked my phone. Still early in what could have otherwise been a long night. But my heart had suddenly filled like a water balloon that had grown too large for my chest.

Isn't that the way it goes? We are so greedy in the moment that we don't keep our attention on the thing we want most. And I wanted Mischa.

The excuse was simple. I went with the flow. The descent into debauchery was never my idea anyway, but it happened.

And in my haste to capture the feeling of unique experiences, I lost sight of what I thought really mattered.

Mischa and I could have been lovers in the park, but we were not much better than strangers at a carnival, each glancing at each other with that knowing smile in a tangential line to our own story's arc.

It all stood like a game of Jenga. Just a tower of blocks to pull from and set our next piece upon, hoping we don't topple the whole. All to blame our failure of the moment on the lapse of another.

I was to blame. You were to blame. We are all to blame for not breaking what could only be broken with action. Calling upon isolation to drink the time away from the pursuit of love, yet unrealized, begets the same failure as stringing one's faith along on tidbits that amount to nothing.

Friendship? Fuck buddies? Both meaningless in the grander sense. Whatever happened to seizing the day? When did it stop being "capture the moment to build tomorrow" and begin to be "forget the reality of the world around us by tuning it out?"

An excruciatingly simple change. An easy lie to tell oneself. Why feign disinterest when you know the heart of a love may be taken in by another the next moment?

From both vantages, the chance between Mischa and I could have been over had Kristen not stepped in. I had to ask myself again whether I was up to pursuing a phantom. Chasing what I hoped could be the final resting place for my own tortured heart.

But the Jenga tower just grows taller, and the old wounds of first love remain. Can we learn? We face the same challenges beneath a new mask every day. Doomed as we are to color the same world under our own light, can we trust others to show their true heart, when we don't dare to? I, like Mischa, was guilty of asking for more than I was willing to give without getting something in return. Would letting the truth out tip the Jenga tower over, or was it already falling?

Knowing at that moment that Mischa's heart may be in it, what did I decide? Not even knowing whether something was truly there, I decided it was worth the chance, and all I had to go on was a look in her eyes and the passing comment of a friend. What more did I need really?

The only thing I knew for sure was that it was a lonely walk under the bright streetlights away from the blasting club music. I told the cab driver where I needed to go, and it drove off, whisking me away beneath the moonlight to ponder my thoughts some more as I watched a new parade of party goers walk down the avenue toward Escobar.

To the camp lantern that potential love is, it casts out a bright beam through the true darkness of a quieter realm. But in pulling us to this campground together, love gives us a choice to either throw ourselves into the fire or watch it build and die.

And the fire surely dies, eventually consuming all of its fuel. But Mischa, I don't ask for you forever. I only ask you for now, and to give yourself to me completely. Drink me up fully as if our love is equal to slaking an insatiable thirst as vampire's thirst for blood. Leaving us breathless, broken, hungrier.

Leave me dependent on your whims. I want to shake when I hear your name. I want to wallow in distress each moment that I do not receive your next text. Give me hope that we might have what others have discovered.

For even just a moment more. I can hold that feeling deeper in my heart than anything else could ever be held. And I won't be the one to tip our tower, but I will gladly burn in the passion of desire.

Come with me, pretty dove. I have no magician's tricks or sultan's treasures. No buried caves or starlit flowers. All I am, you've already seen from the sky. Caught in your web, I can be nothing but yours.

Mischa. I cried out at myself now. Mischa. Why might I have spoiled my fantasies on the idea that they were merely make-believe?

Oh, Mischa.

I am man. And even when you've broken me down to my smallest pieces, I will still be just a man. With no gilded signets. No silver trinkets. Just rough edges that no sandpaper can refine.

And you should hate me. You surely will. For I am too quiet yet too loud. I act with no regard for anyone else. But please hate me only after you've loved me. I ask you this, because in another moment, in another time, you will know with what passion I have loved you from afar.

I look back now at those sleepless nights, cherishing an intangible figment, thinking of our search for a kernel of understanding. For a hope that there may be some real truth to find out there in the universe.

However, we find that there are no great truths or answers. We will forever search for something that isn't there. Is that indeed all we'll ever find? Are we doomed to walk the night alone, only briefly touching something beyond our inner self?

I hope so, because to find a theory of everything would cease to give our purpose to living. And if we were to realize that we are merely what we see on the surface, we might have to come to terms with our incapability to fully grasp the meaning of what we find.

With love, we suddenly break past an old barrier. We achieve a name, and in name only do we truly succeed. For the cycle begins again. The tower can either stand or fall with one move.

• • •

Where Kristen was both a forceful presence and a little on the wild side, Claudette, the other Canadian woman who I became good friends with during the later months in Thailand, had a passionate personality with a bit of a fiery temper.

Claudette was a cute girl from the French part of Canada, who was working at the Canadian embassy. She told us startling statistics about traffic casualties and fatalities in Bangkok.

We bonded over a number of experiences. She joined a number of the outings that I've already mentioned, but it was really a trip to Burma that she planned for a small group of us that split my time in Bangkok into two halves.

When we stamped our passports at the gates to Yangon, she satisfied an international travel goal for number of countries visited that still earns my massive respect. The border had just been opened again to casual tourism, and one of the Dutch guys and a good friend, Mike, had been there in December.

We got some advice from him on places to stay, but the price of a hotel just outside the city had shot up from ten dollars a person per night to seventy dollars in the span of three months due to increased demand.

With no other good option, Claudette, Fabrice and his friend Jason, and I took it. Claudette argued adamantly that I shouldn't share a room with her, which still stings a touch. But, in all honesty, I needed to improve my act. At the time maybe I deserved to be kept at a safe distance with a wall between us.

The girls at Nonsi used to call me the Barney Stinson of Bangkok.

We came in on a budget airline the same week that there was a riot and terrorist attack in the middle of the country. Not a place I would tell my parents I had visited until well after I had arrived back home, stateside. As we came out of the airport, we noticed that Yangon did not have the same density and atmosphere that its nearby neighbors, Thailand and Vietnam, had. The city had a certain mystique in its beautiful and grassy hills and a unique charm.

There were no motorbikes. They were banned nationwide after a tragic road accident. Practically all the cars were painted white, and they were all left-hand road cars, bought from Thailand, driving on the right side of the road.

Surprising to many left-hand roaders, much of the world drives on the right side

We took a car into town and spent the night in a clean place with bathroom fixtures that seemed to date back to the 1920s. Probably did.

The next morning, we had a fairly modern Asian-European fusion breakfast that was a little limited downstairs and prepared to head to see the sights of the main city when my roommate, Fabrice, decided that he wanted to leave our room key at the desk.

He headed over there and smiled at the girl, who mumbled something. When Fabrice was almost out the door, she said it again, a little louder.

"Excuse me?" Fabrice asked.

"Would you like an upgrade?" she asked meekly.

"Upgrade?" Fabrice replied in an exaggerated, excited tone. I came over and stood next to him as he began to negotiate.

"Yes, to the Inya Lake property."

"That was one of the four-star properties," I said under my breath. There were only two at the time, and it had far exceeded our budget.

"No extra charge?" Fabrice asked.

"No charge," she said.

"Yes."

"Great, we will move your bags over to the Inya Lake hotel for you. You can check in any time before 4 p.m."

"Just let us talk it over with our friends first," Fabrice said.

We shared the news with Claudette and Jason.

"This sounds too good to be true," Claudette said as the four of us watched an older, more skeptical couple turn down the upgrade. But after I reminded her of which property it was, one that we had looked at with envy only days before, she decided to give it a chance, and it happened to be one of the best decisions we could have made for the trip.

That day, as we walked the streets of downtown Yangon, we escaped the slow pace and familiarity of Bangkok for the fast-paced, bookish culture of the Burmese. We were passed on the streets by much busier people. We saw bookstores everywhere and children working on forms of art with lights that looked like dreamcatchers.

We passed through some Buddhist temples and then down to the famous hotel, The Strand, where we took a peek at some incredibly expensive art on display. We walked along the river and spied on the locals waiting for the ferry.

The entire town was an old British colony that had basically been left completely intact. Barely a wall had seen any of the damage of time despite many decades of vacancy. We were practically walking through a ghost town with open, inviting doorways leading to dark, deserted hallways.

Four-story buildings from this old English metropolis were overgrown on every level by creeping vines. Trees snaked up the edges from the ground. Roots dug up sections of the pavement.

I watched a small child carry water inside a building with the crashed ruin of an old elevator between a decaying staircase winding around it. The little kid hopped over broken steps with no second thought as I struggled to find a single support for the crumbling structure.

We went up to Chinatown and then to the main market where I bought some candy. It was enjoyable, but I couldn't bring myself to finish it after I gave only a single piece to a homeless kid whose mother was coughing up blood in the street.

Having recently opened, the city and the country were in a state of new beginning, and despite some of the humbling aspects of what appeared before us in that moment, there were many things that the Burmese had to be proud of. Electricity, running water. Carnivals on the edge of the lake, amazing local restaurants in serene settings spread out around the city, and cold beer at an exceptional new pub down by the river.

Our new hotel stood alone on the edge of a long lake, and all four of us took our morning in leisure at a table with a view of the sun cresting over the horizon, directly across the glimmering water. Just inside a set of double doors, there was an unlimited breakfast buffet. Where the breakfast the day before had been fairly standard, we had course after course laid out essentially for us alone.

We went out to the pool and played in the sun as couples staying at the hotel came down to use the tennis courts. It felt like we had drifted into a miniature paradise. For so many of the international students, these excursions to nearby countries would become more and more commonplace. We all raved about each one as we found new worlds to enjoy in the sunshine of places like Laos, Cambodia, and Bali.

Then we were out and about again taking in the world that grew into shape before us. We went out to the Shwedagon Pagoda where the gold-painted structure reflected the candlelight into the night like a halo, and we followed the noise of the crowds to a concert being held in the park near a giant, floating restaurant shaped like a duck.

I miss those moments of discovery that paint the world in pleasant warm hues. So often we make our stay too long and learn that the world we thought was too good was only the same as the rest.

All we really needed was good company, and as we walked along the city's central lake, listening to the open-air concert and watching as the locals hung out in couples, playing carnival games and buying T-shirts, I thought of Mischa and seeing her again. As nice as it was to spend a more temperate evening on this beautiful lake with thick, white lotus petals floating in the water and dreamy hues of blue and green sparkling beneath the glow of little lanterns lining the walkway, I thought of Nonsi as my home away from home. With all of its different cultures and types of people converging in one place, it made for a little island oasis in the swirling, often dramatic world surrounding it.

• • •

Soon, we'd be back in that special place, traversing its heat, its contrasts, and enjoying its simplicity, too. One night Claudette, L, and I would get stuck at one of those mythical traffic stops that make some nights in Bangkok so memorably infuriating. We took a cab from the Nonsi street at the corner with Chua Phloeng like so many times before.

We asked for the Sunrise Tacos on Sukhumvit, and we took the classic drive over the train tracks and back toward a highway exit. When we approached Sukhumvit at the Soi Asok train station, we became stuck in absurd traffic.

For a while, we didn't even notice. I looked up from the laughter and the fun to see that there was a little boy walking between the cars, peddling the treats. When I checked the meter, we had been at the same light for over half an hour, and we were still at least two light changes deep at one of the busiest intersections in Bangkok.

We got out of the car, tipped the cabbie one hundred baht extra, since he would have to sit through the light, and took off into the night to find our thirty-dollar tacos in an otherwise cheap city. Care-free, energetic. We ran through the streets as the heat bore down, and the good company was all that we had or needed.

I could sit at that spot forever, waiting for sunrise as the morning ticked by and the nightclub next door filled up, only to forget the staccato click of the high-heeled "heiress or hooker" game of roulette that developed each night.

chapter five

The Dutch

When we got back from Burma, early in the morning a week later, we joined whatever group was up and relaxing in the Nonsi lobby and, like usual, waiting for 3 a.m. McDonald's to be delivered. If we were lucky, we would have made it back to join the order, but the group almost always ordered a massive tray of fries for the table and any stragglers like me.

My mind may have been stuck on Mischa, but Mike's birthday party was happening before Charmaine and Adib, the Singaporeans, went back home. So, for at least one night, a good chunk of Nonsi's residents would celebrate together.

The next night, we sat out in front of the lobby at the long table that we usually sat at. Maeva set out mosquito repellent candles beneath the table, wafting a light perfume as they burned. I don't remember ever being bitten, but there were plenty of them hovering at the edges of the incense.

Mike sat at the head of the table, which included the Spanish guys and the Italians. We toasted to him, and as I look back I remember all of those happy faces. We were all so damn happy.

Just as Charmaine was saying something about the models that lived at Nonsi, they walked by, and guess who led them out front. Miss Mischa herself. High heels, hips swaying. Her hair swung from side to side. I smiled at her, and she smirked. Guess she had made some new friends.

"You don't have a chance with that girl," Charmaine said.

"We'll see," I replied.

"Come on, Jake. Be real."

"I don't know what you're talking about Charmaine, but I'll let you know how our first date goes."

"Shut up." Charmaine punched me in the arm. "Stop kidding around all the time."

While Mike's birthday celebration advanced into the night, measured by Chang after Chang, my thoughts drifted to seeing Mischa across from me at a table alone at our first date the next day.

"What are you thinking about, Jake?" Mac, the other Dutch guy, asked from the other side of the table. "A girl?"

"It's always a girl," I replied with a smirk.

"Oh, really? Mac laughed. "Please tell us?" It sounded like a question, but he left it open ended. He sat at the other end of the table with the Finnish girls.

I just smiled to myself and turned the Chang beer around in front of me. When he noticed that I didn't intend to respond, he said, "Jake, what kind of girls do you like? Do you like the Thai girls?"

"That's like asking me my favorite food," I said. "I like all girls. American, Spanish, Japanese, Thai. French, Italian. Dutch." I gestured to him and Mike who were both Dutch.

"That's good." Mac laughed harder than before. "Really good."

"What about the Finnish?" Sammi asked.

"Of course. I like them, too."

"Maybe you should have said favorite color," one of the girls said.

"But I have a favorite color," I joked.

"Let me guess? Pink."

"That's my line," said Mike with a smile.

Mac liked to sing songs, and after we sang "Happy Birthday" to Mike, Mac broke into Dutch songs.

"Mac, do you know any American songs?" I asked.

"Some, but I don't know all the words. Do you? Sing us a song."

I smirked. "I can sing 'Don't Stop Believin'.' Probably sung it like a hundred times for Rock Band."

"Hmm, I don't know that one. Can you sing it now?"

"Sure," I said. I played an instrumental from my phone and sang along.

"Nice," Mac said. Everyone else seemed absorbed in their conversations.

"We should do Karaoke some time," I said.

"What's this?" Mac asked.

"It's a Japanese thing where you and your friends go and sing songs from a track."

"Oh, I've seen this. Only, we don't call it Karaoke. Yeah, do you know a place?"

"No, but we can find one."

Kristen and Lorenzo, the Italian, seconded the motion.

The night smoothed off with each clink of cheap beer, and we drifted away from the table until we all found our way back to our apartments. As with each night, I took a cold shower, hoping that keeping the window open would keep me cool enough to sleep the day off.

• • •

Our lunch date became a double date. Four of us. Mischa, Miranda, Finn, and I walked over to a brick oven pizza place called Mama Dolores.

Finn and I had been there before a few times. The Spanish guys, I think, had shown it to me first a little after it had opened. It was easily the best food in our area.

They served a mixture of cuisines and had the best chicken shawarma hummus I have ever had.

The walk wasn't the prettiest and it was one of the areas where we really saw the stark income disparity that existed in places of intense economic growth like the Bangkok area.

As we navigated the paved backroads that were little more than a car's width wide, we avoided stray dogs marking their territory among abandoned buildings that were fenced in by thick cement walls. Some of them had completely toppled while others stood as solemn reminders of the follies of human planning.

Though there were fewer of these plots than the completed ones, they made more of an impact due to their image of failure and loss, cursed to bear witness to the merciless wrath of each day's harshest throw. If we could all be so vulnerable, there would be no great secrets or ruses.

We passed a replica of the White House. We could see it through the black iron gates that marked the entrance to the property.

We advanced along the street in the stark heat of day hoping that we did not attract too much attention from the wild beasts that barked out lonely threats like catcalls from a haunted house.

Mama Dolores came up on the left. It, too, lived out its life in the carcass of an abandoned home. The new owners had converted the unfinished courtyard of the near empty mansion into a beautiful, open-air restaurant at the beginning of dry season. A set of plush, lounge tables overlooked a huge, red brick oven dug out below ground level in the middle. It resembled an empty pool that had been converted into an enormous workspace, where you could watch pizzas being prepared from stadium seats.

While most of Bangkok stood in the sun and wind of an unbearably hot day, the rainy season approached quickly, and the owners of Mama Dolores knew that the storms would be coming. They stopped by to tell us once that an interior restaurant was being prepared.

The four of us ate pizzas and talked. I remember Finn pressing the girls on various topics. He pressed them for opinions on world news and the financial markets while I sipped a cocktail. Miranda seemed all right with it—in fact happy to answer his various questions. But Mischa looked off into the distance, not interested in being randomly grilled.

I sat back against the lounge chair and watched her finger the straw in her drink. We had barely had a second to speak together, and later she would tell me that she didn't have much fun. She asked to spend some time alone together, and we planned to get together for lunch.

Mischa was a good, smart, and ambitious girl who, in all likelihood, had more going for her than me. I felt that there was still some spark that kept us in limbo, as our friendship advanced, but I failed to put all of my ambitions into the strength of that one bond, even if looking back I should have. Instead, although more restrained, I continued my pursuit of the spectacular Bangkok night. Was it a mistake to risk what she may have felt for me, if she felt anything at all?

• • •

The chance for karaoke came one night at the same time as another Bangkok bucket list item was checked off. Mac and Lorenzo, the Italian guy who seemed to be everywhere, led Kristen and I and a couple others to the Patpong area for a Ping-Pong show. Mac seemed to like showing people this particular part of the Bangkok nightlife.

We came to Patpong out by one of the Sunrise Tacos, which stood on the corner of the larger soi and the gay street. This Sunrise Tacos became a more frequent destination as the nights left in Bangkok leisurely dwindled down to less remaining than those we'd already spent there.

We went down a little way past dollar shops selling sex toys until we came to the Patpong night market. Being one of the followers, I looked around at the go-go bars that I never ended up going to anymore, amazed that there was still more to this part of the night-life scene.

There was another ladyboy place on the corner of the road that connected the Sunrise Tacos street with the night market. They were tall and busty and looked too perfect to be women. This place was marked by their blue thongs.

Mac brushed past one of the runners who tried to entice us with menus and led us up a staircase in between two go-go bars to a Ping-Pong show place that he said he hadn't been to before.

We took seats along the stage, and a group of old women who looked like they lived an unkind, tough fifty years began presenting themselves before us and the rest of the crowd. Young girls came over and took our beer orders.

The beers were a little pricey, so we agreed we'd only stay for one. As the show unfolded, the younger girls came back and massaged our shoulders roughly, whispering things in our ears.

The massages were short-lived though because the girls began to demand payment in cash tips for the massages, even before the Ping-Pong balls had even begun to fly.

We all refused, and the girls became angry. Meanwhile, the women onstage began to shoot things with stunning velocity.

Ping-Pong balls were jettisoning out like they had been launched from a dart gun.

In fact, Mac said that he was pretty sure that is what they had done, but all you could see was the woman's sex. He told me this story of a different show in Bangkok where a guy held up a balloon as part of a show, and, instead of the balloon getting popped by a dart, the dart had been shot into his arm.

This show was not nearly as violent. It was barely a show. When we didn't pay up for the massages, the old women on-stage stopped shooting the Ping-Pong balls and started scolding us, too. We promptly left, and Mac complained about the bad service.

Frankly, even for Thailand it had been kind of bad, but we went up past the ladyboy corner and took a left, coming upon a more quaint set of shops that included a barber and a nail salon. Above and behind them was an elevated second level that had a Thai-centric karaoke bar.

We traded off singing songs long into the night, and an old Thai man joined us for a song that he dedicated to his wife. His daughter explained in English that it was his birthday and that we'd made his day. He always liked to come here, and he was glad that he got an audience to sing to.

He sang some 80s tune in a beautifully deep voice that surprised us all.

Kristen noticed that some of the songs had been cut short, but I shrugged at it. We were paying per song, but it had been a good time. We all chimed in for song after song and set the mics aside.

As we left, we couldn't find an active cab. A series of bright pink and green cabs, gone dark for the night, lined the opposite side of the street, so after calling over to the drivers and being told they were off duty, we walked along the street toward the main road.

Leading the way, when I checked behind us to see if anyone had lost the group, I ran into a dummied up cab mirror. The mirror had been glued on with cotton balls, and the group of cab drivers came running over hollering at the top of their lungs. They threatened us in the dark of the night and demanded I pay for the mirror. Since I wasn't carrying cash, I wasn't about to take them with me to an ATM. I stood my ground, backed up by Lorenzo, Mac, and the group of girls' from Nonsi who had come along.

I pointed to the cotton balls and wanted to know why I should pay for a full mirror. I waved over the cops, but they told the cabbie to drive me to the station to talk it over there. Kristen slipped me five hundred baht from behind, and then talked the cab driver into letting me off for five hundred. I gave her the cash back the next morning, and even though the taxi drivers had given us a hard time, the night remained pleasant in my mind.

It's strange to think that I spent so little money to do these things or live out nights like this one in Patpong. Had I not gotten into a dispute with a taxi driver, I might have spent five or six dollars on the whole night, but even as a pricier night, it had only cost me thirty dollars.

Most of us had to stick to a tight budget, so we had to keep to a plan for the group's sake. Even though, we still often enjoyed the lavish richness of the upscale parts of town, and got bottle service to gain entry into clubs. We also had plenty of two-dollar meals of *gai krathiam* at the restaurant next to the hole-in-the-wall down the street.

• • •

No discussion about Bangkok is truly complete without full rumination on the food available to slake one's fancy. It is a common misconception to believe that the best thing about food in Thailand is Thai food.

Thai food is good, but it is best at its cheapest.

The most wondrous thing about Bangkok was that it attracted some truly excellent chefs from around the world who opened their doors in this strangely dissonant city whose grandiosity endeavored to create its own sin. Perhaps not so unique when you think of New York in the 80s.

But here we were in our own corner serving up excellent high tea between drunk nights, world class brunches, and unbelievable buffets far beyond those of Inya Lake. There were places where lobsters were stacked five levels high to crown endless tables.

One of the most memorable streets in Bangkok was Sukhumvit Soi 11. It's probably best known for its nightclubs. It's where many of the small pop-up bars open their doors every night, and while it has its own reputation, it's covered with more models than hookers.

Expensive hotels and apartments line each side of the street. Far more expensive than they are worth for anything other than taking a girl in pumps from Bed Supperclub to a place next door. The expensive apartments of Sukhumvit are so scuffed up, you'd think that they were destroyed with malice and intent.

Levels was a club a few floors up in a hotel on the left end of the street. Across the street was Bed Supperclub, which looked like a giant white pill. It was stark, clean, and held the most model nights than any other place in Bangkok, as far as I know.

We had frequented Levels, and I had been down there a few times for various reasons. I spent more time on Soi 8 for the tailors than any other place in this section of the city, but there were a few good restaurants, too.

One of the most memorable restaurants in Bangkok was an American one that had first opened around the time we arrived, called Firehouse. Firehouse was a fire-fighter-themed restaurant, which served up some of the best burgers in the world.

These things were so massive that most people ate them with a fork and knife. The patties themselves had to be at least a pound of beef.

The place was sparkling, immaculate, cold, and had another treat for us Americans who missed a good burger with cheese. They actually imported beef from Australia and the United States.

I got to compare Thai, Australian, and good old USDA Grade A Prime Choice Black Angus beef at a restaurant just off one of the most famous streets for nightlife in Bangkok.

Mac loved the food so much that we had his birthday there. In fact, we went there more than any other restaurant, the only exception potentially being an Indian one that was hidden away in Little India across town.

One day about two months into the trip, a group of about fifteen of us Nonsi residents descended on this restaurant that could barely fit our whole group. I entered late, so I was one of the unlucky ones hugging the wall as I sat on the bench.

It was fun to see the foreigners struggle to eat the huge burgers and impressive to see cooked beef come out of a tiny, little window at the back like an assembly line. Almost every second it felt like another stellar burger and massive side of fries would be placed by a tiny, little Thai girl on the sill.

As soon as the equally petite waitress would grab the burger, the silver-and-white window would slide shut enclosing the two workers in a pearly white kitchen and hiding their workshop from view.

Everything but their eyes was covered in some sort of white papering or chef's clothes, and I had to wonder at how uncomfortable working in that kitchen might be. Then again, it could be even more air conditioned than the rest of the spot.

I had it in my mind, and still do, that the sterile atmosphere of Firehouse had to do with the constant fear in Bangkok of attracting the more nefarious vermin that plague human life.

The night passed on in enjoyable conversation as always, and when it came time to pay, the Frenchies left early to take a smoke. They smoked after basically every meal, but when one of them happened to forget to pay, I covered their portion of the bill.

When we got out into the street, most of the group had left, but a number of us wanted to stop at a pop-up bar that had set up across the street. One of the times that I came out of Firehouse, I remember seeing this gold digger, Chanel, that I met at a wine tasting with her old beau and who couldn't stop asking me about how much money I could spend to take her out.

An awkward moment for sure, but the rest of the group had no idea who she was to me or me to her, and as we stood out on the edge of the street to get our drinks, I took a seat at one of the little tables that were nothing more than colored plastic kiddie chairs.

For some reason there was a game of Connect 4, and I began to play. Turns out I'm pretty good at the game because I went on an altogether unbeatable streak that ended four years later on the Lower East Side in New York.

chapter six

The Italians

Not to leave a challenge unfaced, our fearless, charismatic, and natural leader, Lorenzo, sat across from me for repeated games of Connect 4. As I defeated him again and again, we talked about the world, and he shared a plurality of insights into human nature that I will never forget.

Cars passed in laconic bursts behind us. The clubs were popular, but our little road was cut off from the majority of the cabs that turned up and away from Above Eleven or down Soi 11.

The drinks were cold, and the conversations continued to swirl around us into larger ones. Lorenzo concentrated intensely, but he was in some strange way outmatched at every turn.

"I had heard you were the best, but now I believe it," Lorenzo said.

"Who told you that?" I asked, laughing as the yellow and red plastic pieces splashed below the blue game board yet again for another match.

"Can't tell you." He smirked as he put in his first piece.

"Why not?" I joked in mock offense and then scanned the group that filled the other colored plastic chairs around us. It seemed no one was listening.

"We have a saying in Italian. You say the sin, but not the sinner," Lorenzo said. "I think that is how it would go in English."

"Huh, I get that."

"Oh, I thought I might have you this game."

"Sorry," I said. "Play again?"

"Of course. I feel like I must be able to beat you at some point."

"Maybe you will. I'm not so worried about it."

"And yet, you continue to play to win," Lorenzo pointed out as he played with a piece between his teeth.

"Would you rather have me play to lose?"

"No, this is better." He rubbed his chin and placed a piece that, in a matter of turns, would result in his definite defeat.

"How are things going?" I asked and drank from my Mai Tai.

"Good," he said, and we continued to play. "I think I've got you."

"Nope."

"Hmm, how are you good at this game? Do you play a lot?"

"I'm not sure I remember the last time," I said as we reset and began to play again.

"Not sure I believe you."

"You don't have to." I watched cabs go by and looked over at the others again. "I'm going to miss this."

"Bangkok has my heart," Lorenzo said, "but let's not talk about the end while we are still so far away."

"I didn't realize you were such a romantic."

"It is easy to be a romantic in a city with so many beautiful women."

"Ah, I agree. I feel like my heart is taken from my chest still beating at every turn."

"You're a weird guy, Jake. You sound like you want to be a writer."

"I've tried…and failed."

"Maybe you have another one in you."

"Maybe." I shrugged. "For now, I'd just like to be a business man."

"Do you want to be?"

"Yes," I said without hesitation, and I believed it.

"I say figure out where you are at and either accept it or don't."

"There's four in a row," I said.

"Let's play again."

"I've got another story on my mind."

"What's stopping you?"

"Time."

"Time is what it is, and whether you want to doubt it or not, a second is still a second from now until forever. If you let it escape you, it will be gone before you can open your eyes to wonder at it," Lorenzo said and looked at me from over the gameboard.

"Maybe you should be the writer."

"I don't plan to be, but promise me that if you ever write a book that I can be one of the characters."

"Sure," I said. "I don't see why not."

"It's a promise then, that you will write again."

"You're a clever guy," I said, "but you will never win a game of Connect 4 against me."

"This is very frustrating."

We got another round of drinks. Lorenzo and I had very similar features. Wispy hair, blue eyes. I had to think to myself, with all of the different ways we viewed the world, just because someone is similar looking doesn't mean they'll view things similarly.

If we looked at all of Nonsi, each culture, no matter who they were had changed me in some way. I decided then to look to others if what I wanted to hear was something I didn't already believe. I wanted to be challenged, and I knew that these people had brought me beyond my comfort zone, resetting the bar that would define the rest of my life.

"Jake, are you listening?" Lorenzo asked.

"What's up?"

"You're barely paying attention, and yet I still cannot win."

"It is only part of my strategy. A ruse."

"Of course." We started another game, and he looked up at me. "Are you listening?"

"Did you have something you wanted to ask me?"

"What do you think of that girl Mischa at Nonsi? The one who is going to Chula. I never see her out."

"Why do you ask?"

"I think she's beautiful. I had heard you knew her well or better than most at Nonsi."

"She's nice."

"I've been intending to go for her," he said.

"Oh, really?" I smiled as we played.

"Do you have any advice?"

"Not that I can think of," I replied, and he eyed me suspiciously. I wonder now if the whole intention of the conversation was to discover my thoughts on her. I still cannot tell if it was to fish out information on her or on me—his competition.

"There it is. I win again," I said and finished off my Mai Tai. "I'm ready to head back to Nonsi, are you?"

"I could go for another game while the night is still young."

I checked my phone. "Not sure if I'd call it young myself. It seems the day's already done."

• • •

A group of us were sitting at the tables outside Nonsi when the challenger made his move. Mischa joined us for what would be one of her few nights out, and when she had just started on her Chang beer from the 7-Eleven down the street (courtesy of yours truly), Lorenzo appeared with an easy sell. Khao San Road.

We had been back to Khao San Road plenty of times during the adventures that turned the BKK days and nights into a dream of forlorn echoes, but this would be one of the last and the best times we would have there.

We took two cabs out to the street and were to meet each other on the road. We came in at that familiar entrance that came off just slightly away from the main road and opened into the same old dollar shirt shops and factory-like foot massage parlors that characterized Khao San.

Filling the street that night were a new batch of wanderers, vagabonds, and explorers. We felt the hot touch of the sun drift away to allow us a moment's respite along the fondly remembered mile.

I had never been down here with Mischa, but we had taken separate taxis, so I was looking for her now. One of my group texted ahead, and we found the others at a small bar off the right-hand side. Mischa sat at a full table, but when our group came upon her, she looked back and gave me that old, shy smile, looking away at the table before her.

Her red lips slipped aside to let her white teeth shimmer in the sparkling light of the hot, white florescent bulbs. A longing ripped through my heart to hold her slender form in my arms and pass the night staring into her smiling eyes adorned in soft, natural colors.

She kept her shoulders down and her hands between her legs. She sipped from a bright-red bucket that was likely filled with Sang Sahm, a cheap local brand of liquor and Red Bull.

I joined another table where I sat myself facing away from her and hoped to avoid flooding myself further with the painful jealousy that I had felt upon seeing her sharing a table with my new chief competitor.

There was a time in the world when gauntlets would have been thrown down but that had become faux pas. Exotic romance in youthful bliss had taken on a less ostentatious form where grandiose gestures were replaced by a callous game.

I had, and still have, no mind to chase an endless stream to nowhere, but then again this was no game of Connect 4. This was real life to me, and to have Mischa's love would have been an achievement like summiting Mount Everest with my shirt off.

The achievement wouldn't be an insurmountable feat, but a feat of such terrific worth that it would only be matched by an epic act with the equal power to touch another deeply. To earn her love day after day, I would require an endless flood of roses. To have her as my one and only would be to forever curse myself to not suffer a night away without wondering after her voice.

I could hear her speak now, light and amiable, with that sly Lorenzo. I quickly washed down my own bucket of cheap liquor, waiting for another while I toiled under my own desire. My head felt like it was about to burst, and my silence became more noticeable, given my usual exuberance.

Desire often becomes a boundary between what we do and do not do. Fortunately, for my impressive thirst for Mischa, the strength of my inhibitions had not imprisoned my idealistic heart.

I knew this would be my own ruin, and even if I had intended for so much good and would taste only a brief moment of it, I would accept that. Regardless of what fate may rest in the fog of days to come, I launched myself willingly into it, expecting only the worst possible outcome.

The true substance of those who are ambitious is more than merely the perception of reward, but the power in the pursuit even when we face potentially insurmountable odds. The voice in my head may say *give up*, but there was more than mere desire in the tense ache that bewitched me.

The omnipresence of hope had captured my reality. The fantasy of Mischa had eclipsed that of any Bangkok night.

My dreams could not paint a clearer picture of the imaginary. It was as if destiny had achieved its whole purpose by sitting Mischa and me just inches apart.

All of human existence had come and gone. All wars waged with the sole purpose of casting each of us in this role. We were characters in a film. Portraits of what it meant to be young and beautiful.

Mischa. Me. The stars were spectators in that moment to the sparks that flashed in the warm night between our ethereal forms.

Certainly, the "what could've been" can take control of one's mind, but in that moment, in that night, you'd have to be as single-minded as the Italian striking fiercely beautiful prose across the shoddy patio table to not feel the electricity pulse between our impatient souls.

The waitress came around again and replaced my red beach toy of a pail with another identical blue one. I examined the handle before drinking greedily from the bucket of courage.

I stole a glance at Mischa and at the rest of our group occupying the scattered tables. We stood and went up to the second floor of the bar after we had all finished our final round of buckets. I got a beer and eyed Mischa from the other side of the room briefly, catching that she had looked my way.

I could see Lorenzo making his moves and wondered what ran through her busy mind. We snapped a group photo of the moment, and in the rearrangement, I got myself close enough to her to split the conversation.

"Would you like to go for a walk up the street?"

"Sure," she answered.

And so, we did just that. We made our excuses and went from the dull blow of a collection of fans to the ceaseless humidity of a Bangkok night.

We walked together down the street, and when we passed between a large group, I put my hand on the small of her back.

I bought one of the roses from the little girls running around and handed it to Mischa who smiled and said something coy.

We walked along a little farther, and when there was a conveniently quiet spot in between rows of shirts, I pulled her away from the open market to deliver a passionate kiss under the open sky.

There has never been a kiss returned with more bittersweet want than that one. Our lips locked, and our tongues danced with such easy rhythm that our souls must have found each other once more after a century in hiding only to know that we would be wrenched away from each other by the weight of our new world's momentum.

I could feel her press her slim torso against me, feeling for me like an eager dancer. And then she broke away, looking out at the street with a soft sigh, and her hand found mine.

"Mischa," I said to break the silence.

"You avoid me for weeks and then this," she said.

"I've wanted you for so long."

"I don't know what to think."

"You're such a wonderful girl," I replied. She squeezed my hand.

"Don't speak. You'll ruin it."

"Let's be together tonight," I whispered into her ear.

"No."

We could have been one that night, I knew, except for whatever stopped her from saying yes. We took a taxi back to Nonsi together, and she kissed my neck to wake me. She bid me goodbye at the lobby.

• • •

In this battle of Khao San Road, I had won. Although Lorenzo's pursuit had been quick and strong, Mischa had taken the cab home with me. My chances seemed better than ever.

My feeling of success washed away quickly when I read my texts the next morning. She flooded my phone with them. We had gone too far. We needed to scale it back.

I put the phone back down with a long breath. I turned on the water to take a shower at the coldest setting and let the day begin to the melody of one of my favorite songs. To give up now would be the true travesty, but I would need to bide my time.

Now there was another Italian guy named Giani with his eyes on her. He was suave, older, and frankly smarter than me. All I have ever been is the product of hard work and opportunity. Some call that luck. I certainly do. Especially now when the windows of opportunity shut and open before me like great saws guarding the gates to marginal gains.

The window opened soon after that night on Khao San when Giani invited a bunch of us out for an epic pool party at Sofitel. Not sure how he heard of the party, but we had been to Sofitel for the pool a few times before. One day, Ketel One held an all-you-can-drink vodka party.

Overlooking Lumphini park, Sofitel's pool had one of those endless edges to it, so that it felt as if you were on top of Bangkok looking out over a waterfall that cascaded onto the vast oasis of Lumphini in the limitless concrete jungle that festooned its surroundings for miles.

A couple vodka Red Bulls with a few of your favorite friends could leave you with a feeling that life had gone beyond the boundaries of circumstance and entered abruptly into a higher form of existence where you ended up with invites to parties with guest lists. But that was not reality.

If only the travails and struggles of youth were shrugged off with such vanity. These precocious realizations may have closed more doors than they opened, but in that moment, all it took was a skirt in the wind for us to forget the pressures of the future.

Mischa entered the party beside a slight, taller, and what would have otherwise been a beautiful friend who stepped in the way of my view. I saw Finn, who had swam over to the edge of the pool, guide her to where we had grabbed couches.

An immediate rush flooded me, and I dipped my head full into the cold pool to smother the flash of heat that spread red streaks across my pale skin. She wore a blue skirt over her bathing suit that caught the gentle wind revealing her toned thighs.

She didn't look my way, but Victor and Clarissa were laughing about something between me and my quarry, so I felt hidden in my obvious fluster. Finn joined us and splashed water on me. I saw Giani step out of the water to greet the pretty ladies, inviting them to join us in the pool.

The party continued as we talked about the passion we found for Bangkok. Everyone had some story to share that night, pieces in an intricately woven design that created the unending feel of summer that enveloped the city.

At the time, there was one of those early internet fads sweeping social media. It was the one with the dance where everyone was acting normal one minute and then they go crazy.

Finn took Mischa up onto his shoulders for the music video, and my heart sank into nothingness at that moment. I couldn't help but feel a touch betrayed by my former best friend.

We splashed and laughed as the music pumped up, and the legend of Sofitel's pool parties would grow over the years, coinciding with an increase in the production quality of their YouTube videos. Finn let Mischa down, and she laughed, placing her delicate, long fingers with blue nail polish against his rippling chest.

Annoyed, I went to grab another vodka cranberry from the counter only to be called back minutes later by one of the Spanish guys. He grabbed me by the arm and beckoned me to return to the pool to take a group photo to memorialize the moment.

I downed the drink and set the glass on a waiter's tray before wading into the cool water. I slicked my hair back and scanned the group that beckoned me to join them with such happy faces framed by the golden hue of the Bangkok sun that hovered endlessly against the skyline.

Mischa beckoned me with an outstretched hand, her bracelet dangling over the water as splashes of water rippled out across the powder blue surface spreading like liquid glass before me.

I could feel her eyes wishing such wonderful things. Mischa lurched forward and grabbed my wrist, pulling me beside her, and I took her in my arms with a smile as the camera clicked.

As we yelled in excitement, my hand drifted down until my palm found her ass, and I squeezed it softly, smirking to her as the group broke after the photo. She smiled back and playfully hit me on the shoulder while I made my apologies for crossing the line, but I had hoped that there was something else in her eyes.

The party continued, and for another night, Mischa left me to wonder what it was that she thought of me—a less than good, more than bad, sometimes affluent, other times cavalier, infrequently largess Wisco-boy.

I wondered then, and I wonder now, if I truly ever will know the answer. What version of me is the one that she could see? I had been so moral and proper for so much of my adult life. Working part time to support my own rent and food money while maxing out course loads was all that I could do in a given day.

Now, when confronted with temptation, I had shown such perverse amorality that I embarrassed myself. Still, that was not truly uncharacteristic of any artist to have found their way to the seedier part of the day.

I had gone to Bangkok to improve my career prospects and learn new things, and in a way I was. I also understood more of what the world was beyond the pages of a book or the blue light of an e-zine. Some capture the intensity an experience abroad's intensity can bring as part of their own life mantra. Most, however, are captured by the intensity, and a part of their own heart is lost rather than found.

I can't say much more than that, as I'd reveal too much of a story left to tell.

chapter seven

The Spanish

T he Spaniard who had pulled me back to the group photo at Sofitel was Gerard. He was studying some complicated engineering masters at Chula but seemed to spend most of his nights chasing Thai girls at the more infamous night clubs that catered more directly to *farang*.

During one of our nights on Khao San, he bought me a little purple wristlet that I've kept since then that says "Yes U Can," because he felt that my spirit infected those around me with that feeling.

I feel like that sentiment captures what it was like to put myself so wholeheartedly into everything that I did. A tendency that has been known to cost me some semblance of would-be pride, but has allowed me to achieve a wide variety of goals.

In the end, it also cost me dearly when it came to Mischa. For the manic-obsessive in me whose romantic and untested fragile heart would attach itself so completely to the idea of the woman Mischa could be and not the young girl that she still was.

Where other loves had failed, ours would succeed, or so I thought, but now to share with you the story of both my success and failure.

The high and low. The soaring victory and humiliating defeat. A battle that I willingly fought, only then I did not know that the stakes we played with were ultimate and the results interminably disastrous. It would be a miracle if I ever trusted another person again, but I did and would trust many more.

Our love and the lies that it relied upon. Our wishes that the future would never come, but the utter impatience with which time took our days and nights away from us.

For years later, when my mind wandered at the intersection of bored and unimpeded, I could not escape that same feeling of helplessness that drowned out what had once been my poetic self, chasing the sweetest flavor and brightest color.

For that was what Mischa was. She was the whitest dove and the reddest rose. Hers was a scent so reminiscent of the flower from which her silhouette appeared that it haunted my silence and could not be wiped away by new conquests.

Both future love and loss, like an imminent curse, would ensnare my heart again in that spiral of self-loathing, which is why I share the story now as a form of catharsis to expunge the demons that I have created for myself, but I am getting ahead of myself and perhaps pontificating too deeply on that which has only partial context as of yet.

The woman in white had driven me mad for months, and finally our shared fondness created a unique opportunity to share the night life together. While, like I said, she didn't get out a whole lot, she began to take more careful steps into the scene that all came to a finale one night at, you guessed it, a night club in Bangkok.

From my very first weeks abroad, the night life in Bangkok certainly shook my small city mentality to its very core. But I'm not sure how it compared to Mischa's experience stateside in Seattle. Seattle wasn't the city that Bangkok was, and Mischa was twenty at the time, I think.

By now, we've discussed most of my favorite parts of Bangkok's night scene, except for one place of major importance—especially to the Spaniards, RCA 25. That place was bumping.

There were a lot of clubs to check out all over Bangkok, but there was only one street and one specific club that really left an indelible mark on everyone at Nonsi. Route 66.

RCA 25 basically only housed a series of clubs that got cheaper as you went along the street. The first one on the right had a couple Lambos parked out front, but the one that really grabbed the foreigners' attention was just about midway down, with blue neon flashing the name Route 66.

The club attracted *farang*, mainly because it didn't require us to pay for bottle service to get in, and the eager girls that chased us, hoping, I think in part, that we'd be gentlemen. What they inevitably learned is that while we may be kind, we aren't much different from anyone else in the world. Still, there was an implied monogamy to us that may have remained an advantage.

Although we came there a lot as part of many different groups, no one loved that club's scene more than Fernando and Gerard. Gerard probably was better known as he had the market cornered on having game when it came to Route 66.

He was single and in Bangkok. By the end of the trip, he knew Thai pretty well and spent, what felt like, almost every night there at RCA 25 that he wasn't working on some project in the Nonsi building's business suite.

One particular night stands out more than the rest. Not just that Mischa came along, but it felt like almost all of Nonsi went along.

Finn and I went over there together, and on this particular night, L was there too with an Aussie friend who visited for the weekend. Gerard led the group, and since Route 66 was expecting to be super busy, they opened up this gated area out in front of their club and into the street.

L ordered us bottle service, so we were sitting on these long, low white couches set around a sleek white table stained by drink rings and what was probably cigarette ash. This was part of L's nightly strategy to get things started and pre-game while letting the club's scene begin to set, but the group split up on the decision. Mischa went into the club with Gerard and most of the girls. Not wanting to look as obsessive as I was, I stayed with Finn and L in the half that sat around the table, putting ice cubes into our glasses and ripping through a few bottles of Johnnie Walker.

Finn talked about something that was happening in the world outside, and one of the French girls sat, listening and lighting a cigarette. I had my back to the club, but I could hear the bass thumping in my ears and chest. When we finished the bottle, and moved back toward the main dance floor and DJ, almost the entire outer area had filled.

L and the other Aussie scouted the tall, standing tables closer to the club, and Finn and I went inside. Two Thai girls stood near the bar, and then they came over to us.

"Hi, I think you're cute. Want to dance with us?"

"Sure," I said, "*kun narak.*"

"Your friend for my friend?" she asked.

"What did you say?" I asked, barely able to hear her speak over the music.

"Your friend for my friend?" she asked again, but before I could continue the conversation, Finn had continued on and began talking it up with a large group of girls across the main floor from the DJ.

"Sorry," I said, then I saw Gerard perusing the outer edges of the interior, dancing one on one with Thai girl after Thai girl.

When he came around, I asked him where Mischa was, and he pointed me to the table right in front of the DJ. He smiled at the girl beside me, who smiled back, and then he leaned into her ear and spoke.

I glanced at Finn getting mobbed by an adoring group of Thai women, who surrounded him, and I smirked. He clearly loved the attention. I followed him to the main floor, and then I saw Mischa near the front, just off the dance floor.

Just as I looked past Finn, she scanned the crowd, and our eyes locked. Whatever was in hers and whatever was in mine, it was the same feeling. She didn't take her eyes off me until I had slipped past Finn and dodged groups of Thai, enjoying their drinks and the music.

There was space around her like her beauty had created a forcefield, buffering the world away. In the soft, neon glow coming off the DJ, her tight-fitting dress shimmered, and the silver of her high heels caught the light.

I had danced at this table a couple times, including the night with Tyler and his girlfriend, but this was the first time I had found a willing dance partner to take in the night.

Finn caught up to us and gave me a look that didn't take a genius to decipher. He took Mischa's friend across the table in his arms, and when my hands patiently slipped along Mischa's hips, she purred and looked back at me with a mysterious grin.

She took a drink and offered me one, then she pulled me against her and danced with her front to the DJ, grinding her backside against me.

I held her dress down and put my lips against her neck to deliver a soft kiss like the one that she had playfully placed against mine in the taxi.

She looked back at me as I went in for another taste, and she tilted her nose up displaying her soft, red lips to me.

Our lips met, and we hungrily forgot the world around us.

The songs drifted, and we only had each other in our arms.

The songs spoke of leaving reality behind, but we held on and wanted to keep it in our grasp forever. Time grew long, and each transition and each beat drop became a marker of the years for which we pushed against each other, searching for something deeper with each touch.

It surprises me still to think what it was that we drank from that made time stand so still. Was that the fountain of youth? Or was it just passion? Or virility? All of these ideas that have ever captured the imaginations of the greatest, worldly explorers but without the same kind of risk. Our risk, we made.

We played with dice on a dim stage in the corner bars, where the faintest of dreams echoed their horrible hope upon us. Even in the clarity of a world so filled with poverty and false faces did we forget to see the obvious before us.

That we were thieves just like the rest. Only we stole the idols of our future from our own minds. For what could we look for beyond what we had already found here together in this carefree world of international companionship?

Mischa kissed me again deeply and thanked me for holding her dress down as her hips swayed with me.

She pulled away for a moment to talk to her friend. She returned to tell me that she was going home with her friend. I uttered a protest, but she put a finger to my lips and kissed me.

"Don't," she whispered. "I'll text you tomorrow." She said something more into my ear and then bit my ear lobe. I could feel myself long to take her right then in front of the entire club, but she touched my chest and rendered me her servant.

I could not resist those eyes, those lips, that voice. She had her way with me, and when she said we would talk tomorrow, I believed her.

Finn and I watched them go, and we went out to see if we could find anyone. Gerard, dancing with some Thai girl, seemed to be the only one left until we found L and his friend dancing outside with a couple girls in bright, pink and white pumps.

We left them to their thing, and so it was Finn and me again, returning home to Nonsi together like we had so many other nights. We walked along the long street, passing the noisy clubs and the Lamborghinis.

He smiled when he looked at me, and when we got to the end of the street he said, "Have you tried this chicken?"

I shook my head. "No. What chicken?"

"The RCA 25 chicken has got to be the best."

He bought me a chicken leg from this cart at the end of the street and handed it to me. It dripped its juices and breading onto my hands like hot lava, and I held it out over the street as I tore into the hot, white meat.

It was like a KFC chicken strip, but better. I'm not sure what the Thai people fed their chickens, but their wings and legs were massive. It was like biting into a chicken breast on a leg bone.

When I finished, I noticed Finn talking to a Thai girl at the corner, and I mistook the girl standing just behind her to be her friend.

"He's good, isn't he?" I laughed.

"Excuse me?" she asked.

"My friend there."

"Oh, yes, he is."

"I'm Jake."

"My name is Emily."

"We've got to run, but I think you're cute."

"Here's my phone, give me your number," she said.

I gave her my number. I took a taxi back to Nonsi with Finn and the rest of the night is blurred.

• • •

Mischa and I met together outside Nonsi, and she called me a chicken for not wanting to take a motorbike to Seenspace 13 with her. She hadn't yet tried Mr. Jones' Orphanage, and she asked me to come with.

I wore a white dress shirt and a pair of shorts with flip flops, and she remarked that I looked nice. Though, just after that she told me that she'd be going to Hong Kong soon, so she wanted to keep things slow between us until after then.

I sat on the back of the motorbike and held onto the grips with one hand, while she sat between me and the driver. I slipped my hand around her waist as the driver started off. We weaved between traffic, and my heart raced. Her flowing summer dress danced in the wind, and she dug her hands into my thighs.

We came to Seenspace, and I paid the driver, then showed her inside the Mr. Jones. She glanced around and twirled, then looked back at me, like something out of a movie. They didn't have a table on the main floor, but they had these little loft spaces, tucked beside a toy train track that ran along the ceiling of the restaurant.

We sat beside each other, and she rested herself against me as she played listlessly with a tin of little, green army figurines. She looked up into my eyes as she talked about what life was like growing up in Seattle, and how she felt like she wished that her time in Bangkok would never end.

She was pre-med and had wanted to go to a good med school, but she was having second thoughts. I told her she should stick with that dream. The world needs more doctors, and she'd be a great one.

We split an à la mode together and dug our spoons into the melting ice cream and dipped them into the decadent chocolate at the same time. A chocolate drip missed her dress and fell on her chest, and I dabbed it with a white napkin.

She looked up at me, with a thoughtful look, and said, "You're a good guy, Jake." She sat up and touched my cheek, then she leaned in and kissed me just beside the lips.

I must say that I was in a pretty good mood after that. When Gerard, Fernando, and this great Estonian guy, Marko, invited me to head to Club Vertigo with them later, I felt like I was on top of the world in more ways than one.

Club Vertigo, at the time, was the hottest sky bar in Bangkok. There were a lot of sky bars, and the most internationally known was Sirocco because it had appeared in a well-known movie like the year before, but Sirocco wasn't even in most BKK kids' top five, nor did it make the top five of a local newspaper's top ten list.

We went to a few sky bars, and we probably went to Sirocco more than any of them, because almost every student at Nonsi had to cross it off their list. This was my first night at Club Vertigo, the highest ranked of them all.

Club Vertigo was on the top of a new, successful high-end hotel chain called Banyan Tree. They had one of those stories that you just lived for as a traveler. It was started by a couple who used to save for half of the year, and then travel for the other half of the year, until they got wealthy enough to realize that the high-end hotels didn't have what they loved most about traveling, getting a feel for the local atmosphere.

We came to Banyan tree and went up to the top floor to Club Vertigo, which looked out in a 360-degree view over all of Bangkok.

We grabbed a photo and laughed over my silly plan to blow the last of my money for the trip on one epic party. I think Gerard and Marko would have been up for it, but in the end, I just kept the money.

"So Jake, I saw you dancing with Mischa last night," Gerard said.

"Yeah," I said.

"Really, nice one," Marko said.

"Thanks, man."

"Did you sleep with her yet?" Gerard asked.

I shook my head. "Not yet."

"Soon, hopefully." Marko smiled.

"What is she doing tonight? We can be your wingmen to help you seal the deal." Gerard smiled.

"Not sure."

"Liar." Fernando drank his whiskey and winked.

"She's at this place called Club Diamond near Mixx club for a friend who has a gig working there."

"Is that one of the models that she is always hanging out with?"

"Yeah." I nodded.

"We should go there next," Marko said.

"Gerard, we've been there," Fernando said. "Don't you have a friend who likes to go there? To Mixx club."

"Yeah, I can see if she is there," Gerard said. "She is a little funny sometimes and a little older, but she has lots of friends and is very fun."

"She's not a hooker, is she?" Marko chuckled.

"No, I don't think so." Gerard shrugged.

"You know, because Mixx Club." Marko drank.

"I know," Gerard said. "You can ask her. Maybe she won't slap you."

"That's okay," Marko said, "but I'd rather hang out with models than hookers."

"I think we all would, but we probably can't afford either," I said and winked.

"Good point," Marko said. "What was it that you said when I first met you?"

"Not sure what you're talking about."

"Your life motto."

I shook my head.

"The thing about rules."

"Oh, right," I said. "There are two rules in life. One that there are no rules, and two that rules are made to be broken."

"She's at Mixx if you want to head over there," Gerard interjected.

"After our drinks," said Fernando.

So, we drank our cocktails in the warm night and watched the blinking lights of the cars and airplanes against the stars in the sky and the lines of the highways.

We got a cab to Mixx pretty easily using an old trick, and we joked while the car weaved its way through the complex web of Bangkok traffic. Only when we got to the Hotel Continental he had to go around to the front.

"What happened?" Gerard asked.

"They were closed."

"This early?" Gerard looked out at the usually quite stretch of sidewalk that was full of people walking away from the club.

"Military curfew."

"What?" Gerard said, and then they spoke a little bit in Thai.

When we got out of the car, we walked around to see if the club was closed for sure, and it was. The cabbie had no reason to lie, because he would have made a lot more money if he had dropped us off there.

I texted Mischa to find out if she was okay. Eventually, she got back to me that she had made it home about an hour before I got there.

That night at Mixx was one of the first of many that slowly changed the complexion of a Bangkok night. When we had first arrived, we would go to a club until midnight and then to another until two a.m., and then to an after-party club until four a.m. and then another after-after party club until six.

Mixx was an after-party club, but the military curfews started to close the whole city down by two. Still not bad, but I had wanted to try more than the one after-after party club that we routinely went to.

But it had been too good to last. L had once joked that nothing good happened until after 6 a.m. Now, we were headed home before we had danced or clubbed.

We grabbed McDonald's on the way home and wondered what it meant to have Mixx shut down before two. In a matter of months, the city would go through something of a military coup, but if those were the first few signals of what dangerous waters lay ahead, we didn't truly realize what lurked beneath the surface of Bangkok.

Only a few years prior the original Central World had been burned down during a riotous uprising, but the city seemed so prosperous. Malls were opening or reopening every other month. All of the streets were full of tourists and Thai almost 24/7, but that's the rosy picture that you see when you first get to a new place.

When you've spent more time there, you begin to see the cracks. Newcomers to Nonsi didn't miss the restaurant, and to them, Cindy, the cutesy Thai girl who staffed it, never existed.

Nothing was that simple, though. There or not or to have or not. When we first arrived, the place seemed so incomprehensibly large, but then the secrets and closed doors began to open, and the veneer of kindness and respect we often received was replaced by a complex array of emotions that began to lay bare with time.

To stay in a foreign nation, with its own customs and intricacies that thinks much less often of the goings and happenings on the other side of the planet than some Americans think, is to ignore that you remain on the outside looking in. To visit is to learn and expand one's own horizons, but there comes a time when, as we've all heard countless times and I repeat again, all good things must come to an end.

• • •

And yet, that time had not yet come for me. There was so much that opened wide as the world and its potential grew into a more matured view of what things began and ended that we were lost completely in the moment.

It had absorbed us so totally that the outer edges of the realm no longer cascaded into outcomes, but we lived for the hot sun that would have once marked only summer days. In January, I had applied for internships, but in March, I forgot what "prestige" they might have once meant.

The nights filled with good food and good company. The days became so routinely unique that the small city Wisconsin that lay ahead of me became just as much a figment of my own imagination as my own dreamy depiction of yesterday.

When or what happened, and to whom or how, ceased to exist on the same plane where I had once concerned myself with existence or its meaning. We were so much more already than we ever would be, but the day would come when, for this manifest mistake, I, at least, would pay.

Mischa, my vision, still, of all loveliness and sweetness, I wish that time has been kind to you since we last spoke. Since we last dreamed. Since the days and nights grew into one and the windows and worlds closed in to be just what we wanted from them.

I do not blame you for the plague that your exquisite honey has become to drown out the day and renew my sorrow. You were nothing but a catalyst to a swirling sequence far beyond our control but unfortunately not beyond our emotion.

If sorrow could again be so sweet. If delight could only for such a brief time be so bitter as to swallow the passage of time in that strange bubble where we alone held sway.

The hallowed line we walked together might reveal itself in a moment of pure chance. We could have it if we wanted, but that inescapable force that gave us our cards also shuffled them away.

One day, bright as any I remember, with the light cascading in solid beams through open squares cut out of the sandstone staircase and illuminating the old, church-style stucco tile that made up the floor, Mischa caught me near the elevator.

I had been running up the stairs, catching two at a time, when I saw her in the corner of my eye, and she whispered my name, floating it to me on the wind. I say it in that way, because that is how I remember it.

Like a soft, insubstantial thing that bent with the whim of some unseen force's fancy. I could have easily been up the next half of the staircase to the fourth floor before knowing she had been there at all.

But there she was. Injured. Tossed off a motorcycle, she said, and I kneeled down to inspect the bandage that wrapped around her leg.

"Are you all right?" I asked.

"Fine," she said.

"Are you sure? Where did you get this done?"

"The Bangkok Christian," she replied, and I did my best to hide my concern having heard plenty of stories from L about the hospital.

Sensing my concern, she said, "It was the cheapest option available." I had already known that, though.

"When do you think you'll feel better?" I asked.

"I don't know," she said, and then she said the magic words. "Why don't you stop by my room sometime and check in?"

"Do you need anything? Is there anything I can get for you? Where are you going now? Will you be all right?"

"I was just going to get some food downstairs, since the restaurant reopened. I'll be fine."

"I can grab it for you and bring it up."

"Okay."

I remember standing in the back corner of the covered parking lot where the restaurant had re-opened, waiting for the takeaway that I would deliver to her door, wondering at all the things that had transpired between us since we had arrived on the same night those many months before.

So much felt like it had changed, and yet we were still almost completely the same. I felt invigorated and empowered, even though maybe I shouldn't have.

I brought her order to her door and knocked. She told me to bring it in. She was lying on the bed, so I placed it on her table.

She had moved since she first came to Nonsi to save on rent by splitting a studio with another girl. There were two beds in the room pushed up against the far wall, and she had pulled the shades on the windows shut.

She had said this was to keep some creep from looking in her room, but it made the place seem dark and a little dingy, compared to the world just beyond the shadowy fabric. She had one light on that lingered over the table and illuminated her eyes, which swelled when they caught mine, the blue at the edges of her pupils turning to a thin line.

We were lucky her roommate wasn't there, and I began to take apart the packaging of her food on the table. I found her a fork and knife and then sat down on the chair. She left it alone for the moment and let herself fall back against the bed with a sigh.

I sat next to her. Awkward at first. I could not help but look her up and down.

"How long is your roommate away?" I asked after the silence had grown longer than the shadows that filled the room's patient walls.

"She's away for the week actually, in Koh Phi Phi," she said.

"Aren't you going to Hong Kong soon?" I asked and remembered that she had wanted us to slow down until afterward.

"Yes." Mischa sighed and tried to turn over, but then quickly gave up. She grimaced and I leaned closer. She looked up at me and smiled.

Something in me was more a man then. Something in me could be what she and I both wanted. For I placed a gentle hand on her side and leaned in to give her the last kiss that broke whatever dam had held in her flood of want.

Inhibitions be damned. Concerns over whatever it was that circled us like sharks just outside our sheltered lagoon became just that. Outsiders. Shadows of the unreal. Unwanted. Unknown.

She, her hands, her body. Delicate, soft, fragile. I strummed along her spine like she was the finest instrument known to man, and she responded in kind, letting out passionate pleas that drifted up into the air like lazy flourishes of a painter's brush.

Her lips found my cheek, and then my ear, and then as I glided my hand to her finer lips, she moaned into me. "Yes, I want you so badly. Take me now. Don't tease me any longer."

She called my name as I shed her panties. Her voice echoing behind me as she wrapped her body around me.

I could hold her entirely in my arms, almost as if nothing was there. Weightless like a feather, but her mind seemed to run like fire.

Begging me to give her all that I had to give. We danced dreamily together as a lotus does in a shallow pond, casting our shapes against the standing mirror that stood against the wall beside the bed.

We looked together at it, and I could see the suppleness of her body against my more dominant size. I lay her back down and went for more.

Her hands dug into my hair and pulled at the sheets of the bed. And when she writhed and cried out and slammed her fist against the bed and pushed herself against my face, like it was all that she could ever want or need, I followed her into the abyss of satisfaction that enveloped us.

She collapsed and pulled me up to her to taste each other's lips like the lovers that we were. Our tongues slid against each other, and she kissed me deeply until pulling away was all I could do to catch my breath.

"This is the last night we are seeing each other, right?" I said what I had thought. The doubts that had always lingered shed in plain daylight before I could keep them to myself.

"Why do you keep saying things like that?" Her arms surrounded me, and we lay beside each other.

"I don't know. I don't want it to be true, but it is though, isn't it?"

"Kiss me and shut up," she said, and her hands found my virile passion. Dancing her lips across my chest, she removed my shirt until those soft, wet little lovers found what hid beneath my pants.

Her dark hair caught the sun as it neared the horizon, casting it in yellow like the center of a sunflower. I watched me go into her.

I filled her and watched her lips overflow, but still she whispered sweet things to me begging me to fill her more and end her lonesome famine.

A soft breeze blew back her hair in the wind, revealing the curve of her chin as if pulled into the encroaching darkness by angry waves in the ocean.

I pulled her near to me and kissed her long and deep, feeling her sink into my arms as tenderly as the shadow of night envelops the day.

And then the night came, and we lost and found each other as the flickering light over the forgotten table was the only light that remained.

The moonlight slipped through the shades of unending horizons, drawing the dwindling consciousness to an echo of memory. Fading shadows danced across stark walls, mirroring our reverie. Her warm body pressed close. Our minds went comatose.

I awoke to feel her hands glide across my chest with simple fascination. Testing for softness where scars stand against firm surfaces. Mine found her suppleness inviting more aggressive strokes until each hand found a curve to again take hold.

The midnight hours passed long ago. As the sounds of our renewed dance grew to each of our own ecstasy, so too did the daylight begin to show.

Through the night we held each other in sweet tyranny, and in the morning, we greedily drank again from the gilded grail.

Satiated by passion otherwise unknown, I could see with each moan of her solemn revelry her eyes grew.

I might simply press the twilight for a miracle, hoping that the moment would never go, but even if we stole pure love from cupid's arrows, we were cursed to return home.

I dove into clear blue water, still shrouded by mystery catching oysters in my palms. Shallow and deep cuts made the work more than regrettable. Each oyster empty, I let them back into the world.

With sorrow and desire, I forced myself to dive deeper down again only to find what I had been destined to retrieve. And in that last, most perfect pearl I had earned a haunting chalice.

To drink from which would poison certain security. It would remind me of a past unforgotten and steeped in stiff regret. But knowing even now what consequences befell me, would I deny for any gain the purity of that bliss?

No.

But, neither could I suggest it. The curse of the ocean's past beauty distracts one from the icebergs that float in wait to drown one's dreams of uncertain but achievable shores.

In all our goals we may have meant to find the silver thread that linked one from an end to a beginning, but to lurch forward is to throw out the past's now unreachable futures.

So easy now to say, cast away the tethers that keep one tied down, but we, then, did not have the courage to plunge any further into realms uncharted.

The ocean grew too dark and stormy on the faded horizon that we held on for only comfort against the breaking waves until in the morning light, they receded.

chapter eight

The Russians, the Finnish & the Estonian

I search my mind now for what reason I had to believe strongly in anything that happened during that fateful spring, and I find again, like I did in Burma, that camaraderie means more than anything else.

I had gone off, in a way, into the far reaches of the world, and to grab hold of something substantial would be beyond any form of reality that I could rightly cherish.

We felt like we had it all, but it was built on patio furniture and empty beer bottles. And yet, I ponder whether Mischa or I merely needed to cast out from our shore and trust.

Maybe, it is simply that we, as people, must fail to grasp at something as simple as that in our youths to learn that we must let go of the things that would otherwise destroy us?

Because what did we really have? Did we have that love, which we longed for? The grand love of all that would put all the other loves in the world to shame?

We barely had a friendship that could stand against the short passage of time. Our Jenga tower was built too tall, too quickly. The blocks had already been kicked out from beneath us, and the drop played out in slow motion.

It reminds me now of how older people used to talk about the 60s and 70s. L had called Bangkok a Mad Swinger's Party where everyone from around the world had let their inhibitions go, and they had called it their Summers of Love.

Well, whatever it was called, it was made up of pieces that when strewn together make enough sense to call something larger than they may have deserved at the time. I can only assume that this is a phenomenon doomed to repeat itself when idle youth strive to find some place where they fit in the world like a glove.

Could we have had more if we tried is the eternal question. But, I don't think it is something that we ever really had. We were ensnared as much by circumstance as by anything. Situational you might call it.

That sounds so cold, but for all I might have done, it wasn't I who ruined it.

What exactly happened? Do you really want to know? Knives spear into the sides of my head as the thoughts return once again to the surface from the deep.

What horror could it be that might have shrunk me down to such a shallow man who cares not to plumb the depths of a woman's heart but to accept one on the merit of a broken smile alone?

Mischa went to Hong Kong for the weekend. Well, it was more than a weekend, but just about. Visiting at the same time from the states was that ex-boyfriend she had mentioned way back in January.

Mischa and I weren't an item that made headlines, and I didn't expect to hear or require any information on her whereabouts. I didn't even consider us dating, but when I woke up one morning to see that he had posted photos of the two of them in bed together in Hong Kong on Facebook…

My heart hit the floor as quickly as a rock falls to the bottom of the pool. I had no words and no anger. The things that I had thought the day before. The things that I could remember myself considering as I had given myself to another person.

They were not deep considerations, but they weren't shallow either. It left me so totally empty that I could do nothing except for delete everything. To purge it all from my life. Photo after photo.

Facebook posts. Tagged things. To block her on everything. But, in the end, I couldn't do it. I logged off and set my phone down.

The only thing that kept running through my head is that she had decided that it was over if it was anything ever at all.

And that was it. It had been built up over months and it had felt so real, and it felt destroyed in a manner of minutes. When I sat up in bed, I could feel that my head shook. I stood up and went straight for a pair of earrings I had bought for her at the Chatuchak market. I unwrapped the little boxes and took one last look at their silver gleaming in the morning light. I promptly threw them out in the trash in the hallway.

So, what have I decided that we did have if we had anything? Lust. I think so. There was a comfort in the normal that we would return to, but a bohemian flavor to the world that panned out before us, evoking within our minds an unattainable romantic feeling that we, or at least Mischa, did not allow to take firm hold.

And in my loss of what I had imagined might fill some insatiable void within my own heart that poisoned my sense of self-worth, I did the only thing for which I thought that I might be able to obtain an equal sense of gratification to the sinking feeling of betrayal.

I went down to the pool to start chasing again after random women with the simple goal of feeling myself released from my inner angst through total sublimation of myself to their impulse.

Welcome back to Bangkok.

• • •

Among many unfortunate aspects of this moment, there was no one to talk to about it. I can't remember exactly why, but I had said something stupid to L, and Kristen was with her new beau in Bali. Finn had moved out of Nonsi to a place up the road, and we stopped talking to each other after that night dancing with Mischa.

That afternoon or one of those immediately following it was the start of Songkran and so suddenly everyone was gone. I alone wasted the days in my apartment.

I barely moved from the bed. I got my meals down at one of the street restaurants on the corner and barely said two words.

I watched everyone else have fun on Facebook, and I thought how much I hated to know that my quiet phone and lack of messages left me unwanted.

There was nothing I could do for anyone or say to anybody that would make their day better. I started to miss home.

What was I here, after all, but a conduit for cash? All I was to do was shell out baht for people far more excited to take it from me than to see me. If Kristen had been there, the lady at the restaurant would have greeted her with exuberance and given us both extra.

But I sat alone with eggs and rice and sriracha, eating slowly and watching the quiet street and listening to some crazy Thai guy guffaw at his newspaper or the chirping kas of the odd Thai group that might take one of the other tables.

The gym and the pool were too far away, and I caught glimpses of people coming home covered in that strange clay and soaked from the ice water.

I lied that I had gone out if I was asked, but I never said that I had been with anyone.

I had this strange feeling that I had worn out my welcome. I wondered when exactly I had, or if I had always been unwelcomed.

I wanted to see someone that I could just sit and listen to, but I had no mind to think for who might be there at the time, especially since the strange way in which we had all joined the fabric of Nonsi's community had disintegrated with the closing of the restaurant.

The reopened version didn't have the same sense of community around it, but I wonder if nothing would ever feel the same as those first days.

Songkran ended, and one night one of the Russian model girls sat beside me on one of the couches in Nonsi's lobby.

She had curled up her legs underneath her body and was staring at me. She had cold, black eyes, and an edgy, under-fed look that struck me as something I once saw in a tough area.

"How are you?"

"Good," she said and after a moment added, "how are you?"

"Fine," I said.

"I think I know you."

"Well, I don't think we've met. My name's Jake. Yours?"

"Sophie."

"Cute name."

She shifted, scowling angrily. "We are going to a night club tonight. Altitude is having a model's night."

"Cool."

"Do you want to come?"

"Yeah," I said.

"Meet us down here in thirty minutes," she said.

I ran upstairs, showered and changed. I remember Sophie, but I don't actually remember the name of the place. At the time, I think it was Neko or Nero, but in place of that, all I could find was Altitude.

Anyway, we went inside together, and they showed their model cards. I didn't have one, but one of the guys had lent me his under his hand, and it was close enough to fool the Thai guys.

We sat down at a table as if we were going to get bottle service, but they brought us out a few trays of sushi. It was decent sushi, and I now realize why another one of the Russians was so crazy about her boyfriend back home.

The budget of a model was so small that they were reliant on things like this to make it day by day. The club won, because the crowd would start the night stacked with tall, pretty people.

The models were just interested in survival. I learned that most of them just wanted to have enough money to follow their own passions in life, and for a lot of them, Bangkok was their third or fourth destination with a particular company.

Only one American girl as far as I know, and of course Tyler's girlfriend, would end up in New York City. Some were fifteen or sixteen and just getting started, but for most, they had potentially met their limit and were winding out the last of their modeling days where they still could.

I realize now that is probably part of me that appealed to Sophie. She was one of the sixteen-year-olds at the table, and I was the older, confident gentleman who had maneuvered around all of these other women.

I listened to the girls chat and drank a fruity cocktail, trading glances with one of the tall Russian girls from St. Petersburg who I had met when she first moved in, Talia.

It's funny how some of these women have burrowed their way permanently into my memory.

Talia, who I knew was in her twenties, pushed me toward the dance floor. Her heels were very tall, so she used me to stand up.

Her slender hips glanced across mine. My hand took up half her stomach, and I could see how much bigger I was than she. Her narrow waist fit in the palm of my hand, and she stood slightly taller than I did in her blue heels. She pulled me against her, and we danced until the table had emptied, and our space on the dance floor became too crowded for our swaying hips to turn.

For so much of the night, we had felt like we were the center of attention, and I remember my favorite song being Rihanna's as we were just that, two diamonds. Me the King, and she my new Red Queen.

As we waited for a taxi to come, she strung out in front of me, unfurling her arm, and I pulled her back to plant a kiss into her and then against her neck.

"You are like vampire," she whispered in my ear. "You dress so well and your teeth." She barred hers at me and then licked at my lips before I playfully bit her neck. "They look like a vampire's."

We shared a taxi back to Nonsi, and she wrapped her arms around me. She put her forehead against mine and stared into my eyes.

I looked back at her and then down at her long legs which she crossed and dangled one heel, tenderly rubbing my leg.

"Tell me you like what you see," she whispered into my ear.

"I do." I kissed her back and we tangled up in the car as I pushed her against the seat and nuzzled my chin into her shoulder and chest and neck and brought my lips finally again to hers.

She laughed out, and when we finally came to the apartment building, we went to her room instead of mine. As we strutted through the lobby, I thought to myself of what it would be like to have a girl like her forever. How fashionable we must look at that moment. Her blue dress and my black shirt; her eyes sparkling and shining in the starlight.

As the elevator doors shut to go up to her room, I began to kiss her again. We had some semblance of privacy, which seemed liked a good excuse even though there was no audience too large for my display of affection.

I let her unlock her door, and then whisked her inside with all the speed and passion of a lover unable to resist the temptation any longer.

I took her on the bed with all of our clothes still on, rolling with her on the bed, and pulled her to my side, kissing her.

She pushed me on my back and straddled me, pulling her dress up over her hips, and I looked up at her dominant figure cut against what little light snuck from the bathroom. I remember thinking that this is what being with a real woman was like.

She rhythmically thrust against me but pushed my hands away when I went to take off my pants. I tried to push myself up to kiss her, but her body was too long, so she leaned down to me, and then I caught her and turned her over, pushing her legs up over her head. Her body was so long and tiny, and her high heels dangled up over the pillow behind her against her splayed yellow hair like two blue jays flying off into a beam of sunlight.

Imprisoned as I was in the way her body twirled beneath mine so gracefully and her soft moaning into my ear.

Afterward, she nuzzled up against me and kissed me, but it felt meaningful and meaningless at the same time. I wanted her again, but for the moment, I could see how incapable I was of delivering.

She pulled it out of me, but I wasn't present for her anymore. I was a tool that night for her satisfaction, and she was all that I needed.

Revenge it felt like, but it wasn't sweet. I had done nothing to anyone besides the two of us, and especially not to Mischa. Mischa didn't care. I may have even proved her right.

I had discarded my feelings for her as soon as they had become inconvenient, or so I told myself at the time, and I imagined I would do the same to Talia.

I wish I still had another chance to go back into that moment and hang onto at least Talia, but I can't do that anymore than I can wish upon a star to find the perfect girl in this life for me.

Talia, please forgive me, I wish that I had been better for you, but there was nothing left of me at that moment in time, and there wouldn't be for some time.

I wonder if other people have felt this way, but I know that they must have. I listened to her as she fell asleep. Then, I kissed her goodnight and watched the shadows play on the walls for hours.

She snored against my shoulder lightly, and I left early in the morning just after she woke up. She kissed me goodbye. I took a cold shower and sat on the floor while the water pounded down onto me, wondering what it was that kept me going at all. As I breathed through the misty water of the shower, I felt the disenchantment with the night life grow.

Had I finally had enough?

• • •

Rainy season came to Bangkok soon after Songkran. It started slow, but the effects seemed almost immediate.

Entire streets would be flooded, and the character of the city began to change as people began to prepare for their shifting fortunes.

Classes began to wrap up, and the days became even lazier.

There was no Mischa, and with no Mischa there seemed to be no urgency left to wander in the once never-ending sun, when it would return if it was still there at all. The rain lasted for days, and we could only spend our time watching movies in the freezing A/C, which kept the humidity at bay.

I took the rejection as something of my own total failure, even if I didn't completely deserve the blame, and in a world too where failure seems both widely accepted and impossible to find.

I searched for something left in me of what had originally come to Bangkok. Some kind of thing that I think was supposed to be there in others' estimations.

I replayed a lot of the old conversations, and I remember one day, the Finnish girls asking me to accompany them to Chatuchak.

I had been to Chatuchak so many times. With my study tour the first time I had come to Bangkok. With L, with Finn and the other Germans, and with the French girls.

In a way, going with the Finnish girls was like closing a loop that had remained open and unspoken. We went out there by BRT and snuck under the rooftops, as the rain had started while we were on the train.

We went from place to place dodging the rain under the billowing shop awnings, and I remember we found corners of the market that we had never seen before. Places with glass doors and display cases like a Manhattan jeweler's.

We grabbed some sticky rice and papaya and ate together under the sinking thatch rooftop. I can still see their happy faces.

We had all been so hopeful, and maybe by then we had all come to know what the true face of the world was even in Bangkok. The smiles were often as false as the prices.

We had been duped for so long that I think there was less than anger there. There was only a certain level of bewilderment. Honesty cost a premium.

We went around to where the pets were kept, and I watched the girls fawn over a puppy.

I don't think there was anything about the puppies that seemed abnormal. Were they victims of an illicit puppy trade, I couldn't know, but it made me wonder if anything ever really changed? Was society really just a chaotic set of dominoes that played out into this form?

Regardless, the puppies were cute, and the women loved them still. They weren't mine and they won't be, but reflected on us as people, it reminds me that we all hold each other to a series of strange double standards, while imagining that we must all be the same, when in reality we aren't.

We spent the entire day there, despite the rain. Despite the fact that it was so humid, and the air so thick with water that my toes and fingers pruned even though my shirt remained dry.

I don't think I could have lit a candle, but I could have written in a journal.

We stopped at a place in the back near the artists where we bought huge fruit drinks and a slightly expensive Pad Thai. It was a lot of food, so it seemed like a decent price.

At the back of Chatuchak, there was this artist I had seen a few times over the course of the year, who occupied a large open space, like a private art gallery.

He depicted the world in an idealized hand, coloring provocative pictures of women of the night in the style of old woodblock prints from Japan.

I found that it captured that surreal aspect that we lived on in those early days. Some might call it objectification, and they would be right too. Maybe what we both saw was right, but from a different perspective. Same, same, but different as the Thai would often say.

It certainly is an objective to consider a woman a great romantic obstacle, but then again what would we be if we didn't have relationship goals. A species of creatures without purpose to life?

I don't know. Perhaps that is too deep a conversation to have over the portrait of a geisha? Perhaps that is the only conversation to possibly have about one.

I do think it was strange to see how we, Americans, could be so different. I was a shrewd negotiator. I wouldn't take something unless I had gotten at least 50 percent off. Even on ties when I could have paid full price.

I remember buying ties from "Tie Land" and telling the salesman that I would pay fifty baht. Fifty for the ones that I wanted, instead of two hundred fifty. I ended up paying four hundred for four and argued with him that I was buying on volume.

An American couple, like many others, took a different approach, arguing with other *farang* that they didn't care to negotiate, because they didn't mind paying full price. They could afford it and felt like they were giving back. Sure, but I couldn't live with myself to not haggle.

I should've known then that I was turning. Turning at least away from whatever it was that I had been before I had come to Nonsi. The after-effects of the trip would be subtle, but forever enduring.

"I heard you have a girlfriend now, Jake." I remember Sammi saying this at one point to make something better than small talk.

"Not really sure you could call it that, but yeah, I guess. I'm seeing someone. How'd you hear or from who?"

"It's just been the talk. I heard she was pretty. I always pictured you with a pretty girl."

"Thanks, Sammi. I wish I could say it was a thing, but I'm not sure I can yet."

• • •

Okay, so I kissed and told, but I couldn't live with the memory. It burned into my brain until I put it to the page. Is it an incredible true story or just a normal true story that we as people live out almost every day?

To say that I acted well in the aftermath of what had been one of my life's most crushing moments would be a slight overstatement, but I wasn't so bad at first. I probably acted better than what I would have expected of me in a way.

Whatever positive transformations that I could relate to you crystallized one night at where else but a Bangkok night club? We had been out to Ratchadapisek a few times and most infamously for ice hockey in Bangkok, but it was one night at Soi 4 that would be especially life altering.

The Estonian, Marko, and L got it into their heads that we were going to head out and bar hop for old times' sake, starting at the cheapest set of night clubs that we knew of.

The cab dropped us off in front of the 7-Eleven, which was a part of the parking lot, but opposite of the night club complex that housed a few different places, each with essentially a different theme.

One of the more interesting ones was a heavy metal club on the left. Being a metal-head myself, I enjoyed it the time we went there, but it was deader than the zombies the songs screamed about.

I stood out front of the 7-Eleven while the guys went in and poked around for some tea or something to eat. There was a little table where a few girls in heels, who looked like their night was already done, ate some hot dogs.

A street ran up a slight incline behind them, and I saw some Thai girls walking along there. A couple cars pulled into the parking lot, which was already packed at ten.

L came out of the 7-Eleven and asked if I wanted some water. Seeing he had bought me one, I drank it and tossed it in the trash next to the hot dog shop.

We crossed the lot. In those days I had started to dress down a little bit more due to the rain, and so I cared little about my scuffed-up shoes or my worn-out white shirt that had made it through at least half of the days at Chula with me.

L grinned as he led us up to the club in the middle. He argued for bottle service at a table, but they were visibly over-packed for the performance of a live, local band, and could only give us a spot at the far bar. There were two long, thin bars on either side of a massive open floor of tables.

We walked along the dance floor, scoping out the tables, and we were slightly disappointed. We got a bottle of Johnnie Walker, and the plan was to kill it and get out of there before eleven if a large group of girls didn't show up.

We split it into three glasses and mixed it with tonic water. I couldn't get it out of my head that the night could be a good one, and I scanned out over the crowd like a hunter, assessing prey.

There was a table to the left with a few cute girls. They were with a few guys, so it seemed like they might be taken. One of the girls eyed me at length, so I wondered if I had a shot.

I slammed my whiskey and poured another. L and Marko took off to chase down some leads at other tables, and I watched the band while the whiskey went down easy.

It seemed like they had been gone only ten minutes when they got back, and L looked at me like I was insane.

"What did you do?"

"What?" I asked.

"You killed the bottle on your own," he said.

"Huh, I didn't even realize."

"You're paying for it," he said.

"All right," I said. "What's the game plan?"

"The crowd's pretty shit, so let's take a sweep and see if anything sticks and then head out to Escobar or Mixx."

"Sounds good to me," I said.

Marko grinned at me, and the details started to get a little fuzzy. We circled the tables and none of the girls smiled or made a move, so we went out to the door.

"I got to take a leak," L said.

I could tell that Marko didn't want to leave as he danced with one of the Thai girls. I wasn't sure we should leave either, since we were supposed to meet Mike and another American from San Francisco here also. But they hadn't showed, and when I checked, it was almost eleven.

L came out of the bathroom and asked if I was all right. I nodded. I could stand. I could talk fine, and I could walk in a straight line.

"Good enough for me," L said, but just as we went to the door, one of the guys from the table with the pretty girl, who had eyed me, showed up.

"My friend likes you," he said to me.

After a brief conversation, we were headed back to their table, and L looked at me saying under his breath, "Dude this is just like that story I was telling you about."

I nodded, and we got back to the table. They gave us some drinks. They had bought a round or a pitcher of old-fashioned whiskeys. L started dancing with this cute girl while the one who had eyed me from across the club started grinding up against me in her pretty green dress.

The gay friend, as we referred to him, kept filling up my old fashioned. When L was getting tired of playing cat-and-mouse games with the girl across the table, he signaled for us to cut loose.

Just as he did so, Mike and Cisco showed up. The girl I danced with switched over to Mike, and L's girl went with Cisco as the drinks kept pouring. We said cheers and danced, but Marko showed back up and asked if we were checking out.

L nodded. I agreed and set my glass down.

"He doesn't look so good," Marko said.

"What are you talking about?" L asked. "He's perfectly normal."

I shrugged and went to the front glass door. For those of you who haven't been to Thailand, the doors open both ways and have a little lip on the bottom that the door sits on top of.

In my drunken haze, I forgot the lip, and when I tripped, I didn't even make a move to catch myself.

"And, there he goes," said L.

"Told you he was done," said Marko.

"What are we going to do with him? Put him in a taxi and go?" L asked.

"You're the one who got him drunk," Marko said.

"He did put a lot down."

They moved me up and into a taxi. Marko went back in to chill with Mike and Cisco, and L got into the cab with me.

"*By ti Soi Chua Phleung khap, throng bai.*" L directed the driver and then he turned to me and asked, "You gonna be all right Jake?"

As the car ducked through traffic, it became clear that I was not.

"Whoa, open a window!"

L helped me turn my head out the window, and I chucked out what I could as far as I could. It splattered over the outer door, sounding the same as rain does when it first splatters across the windshield.

L argued in Thai with the driver about who was going to pay for it (us) and how much. We got to Nonsi, and he called the little security guard over, who had both welcomed me to Nonsi and seen me in all my usual uppishness, to help out.

Remarkably, I didn't get any puke on me, and the security guard was able to walk me over to one of the Nonsi tables where I waited while L finished arguing with the driver and in the end paid an extra thousand baht.

The two of them talked over me and decided they would need them both to bring me upstairs. It wouldn't be the Bangkok Christian tonight.

They got me up to my apartment and used my key. They helped me into the shower, and then L told me to take a cold shower and get to sleep.

I sat down in the shower.

"Dude, you got to get out of those clothes."

I shook my head and tried to stay upright, resting my head against the wall. I could barely control my limbs.

"Take off your shirt," he said. The security guard waited in the door behind him.

I took off my shirt.

"Now your pants," he said.

"No," I said.

"Come on man. We've got to make sure you don't die."

"No."

"Take them off," he said more sternly, because it had worked with my shirt.

"No, leave me alone," I began to yell.

"What the hell are you doing?" he asked.

"Nothing," I said.

"How did this happen to you man?"

"Mischa," I said.

"For fuck's sake. What are you trying to do? Kill yourself over some girl you just met in a god damn shithole like this?"

"It's not a shithole," I said.

"This? This is a shithole. It's been cleaned and polished, but you've got a penthouse waiting for you at the end of your fucking life. Don't waste another thought on a girl like that. She's nothing. A shroud. A mystery. Girls like that only exist in your mind."

"Leave me alone," I said.

He put on the cold water of the shower, traded shrugs with the security guard, and he left, letting the door slide shut behind him.

L said something from the other side of the door, but I couldn't hear it over the water. I heard the door close, and the light flickered overhead.

The water began to pour over me. I was alone. I fell in and my head swam.

I needed to wake up, but I couldn't.

The cold water poured over me, and my head felt like it weighed a million pounds. I tried to get up, but I couldn't. I was stuck lying there, but my stomach turned around and around like it was a planet shaking under tremendous seismic force. I could feel my lips begin to submerge beneath the water, pooling in the bottom of the shower, and then my nose, sputtering as I tried to breathe.

I convulsed and shook, but nothing came out of me as I writhed on the floor of the shower.

I wiped my hair away from my eyes and put a palm down on the smooth tile beside me. The door was closed, so there was no risk of Maeva seeing me in this state.

I got myself first up onto my knees, coughing up water and whatever else would come. I shook in the water as the rivulets ran along my back in streaks beneath the pounding sheets.

I tried to get up farther, but the gravity of the world didn't work, so it was just me and my hands and knees. My head hung down as if my neck couldn't support it with its new weight.

I crawled over to the sink and found my toothbrush in the cabinet underneath. I propped myself up by my elbows, and I shoved the back end of the toothbrush into the back of my throat.

At first it didn't work, because I missed the back of my tongue, but then I figured it out and like releasing a civ, more wretched poison began to stream out of me.

I turned away from the sink and pointed myself at the toilet as my body shook violently with each blast that projected from my insides and into that old porcelain throne.

When the vomiting stopped finally, I surveyed the bathroom. My head didn't feel as heavy. I flushed the toilet and looked for my toothbrush. I cleaned it off, and then felt my stomach rumble.

I repeated the procedure this time starting over the toilet until I felt even a little bit better. I cleaned off the toothbrush, washed the puke down the toilet, and then cleaned the sink.

I put the toothbrush away and ran my head under the cold water until the stench of puke was out of my nose. Then I crawled into bed in wet jeans.

The next morning, I woke up feeling like nothing had happened. My phone and wallet were fine. Someone had taken them out of my pocket and put them on my desk.

Nothing was missing. Not even a small bill.

The light of the morning sun crept through the window free from a rainy day, and I went down to get an American breakfast at the new Nonsi restaurant before L woke up.

chapter nine

The American

Perhaps not oddly, I felt strangely reflective after that experience. In a way Bangkok felt over. A storybook closed in on itself, but maybe it was never really like anything had happened at all.

I had no photos. I had no movies. I had no records of the events that had unfolded except those that I carried in my mind.

I was hurt, but I had brought upon my own destruction with each night that I escaped from the world I knew for the "surreality" that Bangkok provided.

So few things had been left undone. So much more stands out now in my memory as being important to me, but in a way empty and void of any real meaning.

I wonder if that's why we return again to our work to see whether the depiction of what prevails in our minds matches what flows into prose on paper.

I can't know for sure. I just remember knowing that it all felt like it would never really end, but things had kept on going and things had kept on ending.

I remember walking up the street for a massage one day at a place around the corner from Nonsi, sort of where Mama Dolores was, but on a different route. The same route that went down to Lumphini Park where I went running a couple of times, overlooked by the Sofitel pool.

Well, I got the massage at this cheap place that one of my friends recommended. Can't remember who. Probably L, but I'm not sure I can credit him with the discovery, and it took me back to all the other massages I had ever received in Thailand.

It was two hundred baht for two hours from the oldest masseuse I had seen yet, and as I lay on my stomach all I could think about were all the people that I had gone for massages with while in Bangkok.

There was that time the year before at Divana, and I had always wanted to take a friend like Finn there to show him what a massage could be. Only we went to places on the same street that I was on now and got these weirdly small boxers to wear that were practically see through.

There were times going for massages alone and with L too, and almost every time I went, I remember being propositioned by the masseuse whether she was young or not.

Whereas I hear so often from women that it is us men who make these advances, I can tell you now that I never accepted even when this busty girl in Vietnam pleaded with me to pay her later and promised I could play with her naked body. I still said no.

The old masseuse with strong hands went over my back, and I eventually fell asleep, but not before I had gone through all the things that had come between me and some of the best people I had known. I couldn't help but wonder if I had done something wrong on Finn's or anyone else's account.

Had I crossed a line that didn't involve Mischa? One night a close friend of Finn's had gotten super drunk, and I had helped her get into a taxi after she tripped on a ledge and dropped a glass, while he watched from afar. Had he been jealous?

I was brought back to reality when even this old lady was asking if I wanted her to give me a bit of extra, and I said no.

But, for some reason, it also reminded me of Maeva, and in thinking of when we first met, I had also to think of Mischa and my heart grew heavy and distraught.

Was there ever anything I could have done? Mischa had no idea that I was going to sleep with Talia. It was highly likely that she didn't care, and she, after all, had her own life to focus on.

We, or I at least, had gone for something which in all true intentions could only exist for that slim moment that had appeared, and in that imagined love, I had been lost and could not escape.

I went out to a famous used bookstore alone and with Kristen and L, and I met a new girl almost every time I went, but Talia still texted and wanted to see me.

For a time after Mischa, both failure and success seemed to run through my head to fill it with self-doubt, but now looking back, I'm glad I had that tower of blocks.

That night with Mischa was seared into my memory, and I could only think of what had transpired as something intangible and unreal. I had wanted so badly to have a reason to say that this is my place or that this was my girl, but I could say this was my place and for a moment, she was my girl.

Only it was merely a whisper on the wind in the night that faded from glory to nightmare as the stage lights switched to cast their eerie glow on only us.

We were nothing. We were all to blame. I could see it now so plainly that there was never any chance of us coming home, but I could only wonder if I would do it again all the same.

I still don't know the answer. I felt the lecherous, old fool, already, as these women and girls asked me to do things to them for money. They were sole proprietors, and I was whom they hoped would be an anxious solicitor.

What they expected out of me I am not so sure, but they had no reason to believe I wouldn't live out their own fancies.

I was a bit player in the Bangkok drama, and if I stayed longer then I would be a more than minor character. Unfortunately, I was cast on hopes alone and soon the director realized that he could not alter the soap opera's lines any further to keep me on.

My popularity could have brought on a revival, but there was ever another American to fill my shoes. Without a doubt they would do it and potentially do it better.

But for so many I could be what they had seen America to be. Wealth, prominence, and with a penchant for the finer wine that drips from the most tender of lips.

I guess that is what I had given up to change: a former vision of myself.

• • •

Soon, I was accepting any invitation to leave the city for a weekend or a week, just to take a break from the routine. I was tired of the thick fog of smog that hung over the city, the constant rain, and the worry that I might see Mischa between towers.

I made up with Finn over a beer, and shortly after, the Germans and I went out to Chiang Mai, where we would stay at a small inn and enjoy Khao Soi for the first time.

One day, we went up into the hills outside the city and rode elephants through the trees, watching them crush full-sized trunks and munch on leaves, and as we came back out of the woods, the morning sun crested over the hills and lit a slight misty glow on the horizon from a soft rain the night before. And then we headed back into the city, thinking of the tender sorrow and wonder for the tragic lives of the magnificent beasts.

That night, we went to see a Muay Thai fight at the center of the city. Now, I have been to a couple fights, but there was something specific about this one that stands out stronger than any other fight that I have seen. Maybe a fighter like Mike Tyson could put on a show like this before everyone knew his name and had learned what to expect. It all gets down to the core of our human condition.

There were two schools pitted against each other. One, the blue team, and the other, the red team. Now, we, being white and *farang*, who could barely speak enough Thai to order at a restaurant, had nothing to decide what team would win a match other than look and color.

The first fight seemed fair enough, but there was something so insanely maddening about the guy in red team's corner. He looked about as smug as any prick could get, and as they fought, I kept hoping the blue team guy, who was in slightly worse shape, would beat him into the ground.

Now, while this was a pretty fair fight, this wasn't blue or red team's best fighters. Those were saved for later rounds, and for the first few punches and kick exchanges, the blue guy seemed to have the advantage.

He delivered his punches well and was able to land solid contact while the red guy had put in a couple attempts at landing a roundhouse a la Chuck Norris that the blue guy easily dodged.

Only when their second round started, blue guy went in for a punch a tad late, and the third kick knocked him out cold. He slammed down on the mat so fast that they had people from the edges of the ring rushing in to make sure he was still alive.

Red team wins.

This confidence became characteristic of that whole side, and there were four fighters. In the second bout between two female fighters, the blue girl won, and I thought for a brief moment that blue team had a chance overall. In a tough fought match, the girl in blue landed enough punches on the girl from red team that she sank into the ropes.

Beside it being my favorite color, I also thought that the red team guy in round one had gotten lucky. Well, short news is he hadn't.

The next two fighters came out, and it was clear that the blue team guy was bigger and stronger than his teammate. Unfortunately, mister red team was built like a freight train outfitted to cut through ice.

The blue team guy did practice jabs while the red team guy hung his arms over the ropes with a smile. Goliath was cocky, I thought, and isn't that the classic truth of it.

Mr. Blue Team may have an advantage in speed, and he was taller. Mr. Red Team wouldn't know what hit him.

The fight started. Blue team guy threw a couple body shots and forced red team to dodge. He gave an opening, and red team put one punch to the head and knocked him out.

The next fight was even worse in terms of match up, and I felt morose, sick to my stomach, thinking about blue team.

They never had a chance. Who were they and why were they fighting here? They were so overmatched that it was barely even worth fighting. The best fight had turned out to be the girls' in the second match up.

Well, over time it got me to thinking about David and Goliath. Goliath appeared to be the stronger of the two, but he was merely a challenger to be trotted out and handled.

David, with deadly aim, was likely the fitter, and even if he was not tested as substantially in battle, David had put in the work to know better the odds. Goliath could throw as many practice swings as he wanted into the air, but David could afford to look as smug as he wanted to. He knew that he would win the fight. Smart money picks him every time.

In the world today, we want to look at our own lives and point out the obstacles that we've overcome. We want to demonstrate our ability to lead meaningful lives by sharing what it is that we've struggled against.

I could do that. I could share more substantial secrets of my past, but to what end? There is no award waiting for me at the end of that mono-color rainbow. That's a falser idol than the shields of past gods and a deeper moment of self-worship as self-aggrandizing than my own vanity is now for me.

We and our heroes are not struggling to overcome odds that are against them. They are the stronger forces and struggling only against the weight of their own hubris to cast off their past and lurch into their future.

Are the best of us red team? Asking us, no, challenging us, the blue team, to do better, or are they something else?

They call on us to believe in things that may be better rather than the same again. And sometimes, better is the same, but different. As the Thai like to say. Same, same, but different. There it is again. And we as people might be better off accepting that to earn a share of fame today could mean that we lose our chance of eminence tomorrow.

• • •

A couple weeks later I took Talia to Koh Chang, an island on the northeast of Thailand's coastline, near Cambodia for a weekend.

We took a snorkeling trip that went out to see two islands further out in the ocean. The water was a beautiful clear blue, and despite any fear of what might lurk in the open ocean, I dove in and held my breath to free dive a slight ways toward the coral.

The vibrant colors of the schools of fish played in the strips of light that fragmented through the water around the swaying shapes of the coral.

When we came out of the water, the sun had burned our backs, but we saw two things, contrasted against each other in that bright omnipresent sun, that further changed my perspective of the world around us.

Out on the spine of one island stood one of many palaces of the king. A vacation home that he had not been to for years, but that staff regularly kept clean. The green palms framed its white walls and red rooves like the most luxurious vacation resort in Hawaii.

Across this bay-like area of the water, on the other island, built at the end of a large beach against a natural corner in the mountainous outcropping of the ocean island, stood another structure.

The ill-fated dreams of a financier rested in the white sand. Blackened and hollowed out like the abandoned projects of the millionaires doomed to rot in Khlong Toei.

Transportation to the island alone had grown too expensive, but the walls and roof still stood. Only there were no doors or windows, and the concrete surface of the building had become so black that it hardly seemed appropriate to leave it there.

Just like the decrepit builds, hidden behind cement walls that had been hollowed out by the elements near Nonsi, riches had been squandered in the pursuit of some dream to live like royalty on the budget of a pauper.

It's not for me to remark deeper on that silent well-maintained castle on that island, but on the other hand, that faded hulk of the businessman's dream? Isn't that so inglorious to tempt fate in seeking to prove oneself as more than mere man, but at the level as superior as one's king. I don't pity the failure.

And, others will chase their own destiny even if it ends in a burnt and hollowed out husk, but he, the king Chula, brought the whole country up and at least in this case, to have a throne for him was to allow Thailand, as one, to build a shared future.

I had desperately but unknowingly needed a break from the city. It had grown or morphed into something that wearied me more than I realized.

Perhaps it had always been like that. I just didn't notice the rose for its thorns, but to call just any flower by such sweet a name is to invite my own moral disaster.

But then again, the significant moral conundrum fell upon me whether I wanted to avoid it or not. Who is David? Blue team or red team? I have my own answer, but maybe it's best for once to return to what has always been one of my forgotten great strengths, silence.

I realize now that the lesson taught to me then is that I would return to the United States having found Mischa, but without having to feel as if I had ever really met her at all. The experience could come and go, and I could let it rule me or build me depending on how I interpreted the outcome.

That interpretation is still out there to decide. Are our Jenga block towers destined to collapse and fires smolder into ash as we self-destruct on our own fuel no matter our intention?

And, if lucky, are we only to build sand castles as we watch the ocean, where the glorious ships of the few who could devote themselves to a life of their love sail beyond the curve of the wave?

Maybe all we do as we grow older is learn to know when to cast off and chase or that there was never any winning to begin with. Do we settle into our roles like the sediment building along the edge of the ocean floor?

There is no world where those who surrender their fate to the whims of the moment, shall not be served vindication in watching sand castles fall at the first break of the softest wave, bringing the evening tide.

Am I a good person? It's a question that I at least ask myself and wonder if others may ask their own reflections in dark mirrors. I don't know. I don't know if there is ever a correct answer to this question, but I believe we can change.

At the time, I never thought of myself one way or another. I just tried to be a person and to find a place between what made up those around me. Now I wonder what is it that we hide? Our dreams?

I only believe strongly in this. That anything worthwhile can't be done for one's self.

No amount of money or fame will guarantee that you are anything more than a song of woe caught between two infinities crashing against the stones of your hopes to watch the tides rise to let your ship take the ocean.

But whether the tides rise or fall, and whether it is yours or any other ship to set sail, the ocean remains. Forever deep and forever wide. The horizon line always there to hide what you cannot see.

To explore its depths is to answer no great questions, but to touch the surface of the sky is to begin a new line of questioning.

Can we? Can you? Yes, you can.

chapter ten

The Swiss

Finally, my emotional tether with Bangkok had been snapped, but that had nothing to do with what Bangkok needed. As far as I'm concerned, it had always been done with me. It never needed me. It was a city. Not a person. Not a life, but a hub of activity.

A meeting place. A waypoint. A stepping-stone that helped one cross the dangerous river that could pull one beneath the water forever.

I didn't want it to be that way. I didn't set out with the intention of focusing on the journey's end, but the journey would end regardless, and I didn't have a say in that.

I began to listen to the old songs that I listened to at home, instead of those that moved me in the club to seek another body for momentary comfort from the abyss of the future.

They spoke of love and loss in a way that reminded me of the perspective that I had gained. Led Zeppelin became a constant companion, and I knew that I would leave Bangkok.

But it was not anything specific in the end that had done it. That had separated me from the person, living in each moment as if it was infinite, and the one that looked on to the horizon ready to set sail home. I knew now that I had come with no expectation, and everything had been icing.

The city had been the ruin of my former self and for another self, a proving grounds. It had given me a skill that I needed to acquire to move to the next level, but also not the perspective to know when it would be needed.

The spring was finally over and behind all of us, and I could spend all my days looking back, or I could move on and enjoy new adventures.

And yet still it went on and goes on. The Bangkok days and nights. Although now, for me, it was merely a victory lap. A loop stuck on repeat as the things I had experienced slowly evolved.

The newcomers to Bangkok saw the same, bright world that I had setting out, and so I think it was only I who changed in how I viewed it. The days and nights were still there for the taking.

I moved in with a friend of mine, Nic, from Switzerland. He was really the only guy from Switzerland even though Fabrice, the German guy who went to Burma/Myanmar with me, also went to school in Switzerland. They were both good guys, but Fabrice, like Finn, had moved out of Nonsi for a better, nicer place.

I moved in with Nic who had a much nicer apartment on the top floor, and for the last couple weeks or so, I slept on a cot that we got from management and set up with my sheets and stuff on the floor in the corner of the living room.

He didn't have to split the A/C budget with any French girls, so we had a lot more A/C, though we spent very little time at the place.

I finally went with Nic to play pick up soccer on the other side of the city at an Arsenal youth soccer facility.

We went through the facility and the locker rooms to the back, to play in these large indoor cages. When we got there, the group was setting up on these benches on the near side. The field was a little larger than a tennis court and had full size goals.

Nic introduced me, and the group asked where I was from and what I was doing in the city. I told them I was from America and had been studying abroad at Chula until classes wrapped up a little bit ago.

Most of the group members were English. Bangkok had a pretty healthy sized population of Englishmen, but there had been only a handful of English students at Chula and none at Nonsi.

The game got going, and luckily, I wasn't the worst one on the field. Every year I've played, I've gotten a bit better, and I was able to make good passes and get a couple goals. The games went well and were closely fought.

We played after dark, late at night, and I think there were a couple times that Gerard and Marko came out to play with us. I don't think Fernando was much of a soccer player.

The Englishmen were disciplined and passionate in their attack and defense. We traded goals sparingly, but the passing and communication were good.

Thankfully, I put up a decent showing. I could get a good through ball going, and I had a good medium range passing game that made for some efficient trades down the side or diagonally across the middle.

Unfortunately, at the time, I had almost no skill with the ball in front of me, and I played an aggressive style of defense fit for a stingy cover defense.

It worked out well for the most part, and I found most games I could hold my own cleaning up at the back end by making good standing tackles and sending the ball to a forward teammate.

They liked to joke that they had thought all Americans sucked at soccer and that I wasn't so bad, but it remained clear that I didn't have much more to show. I later developed an eye for goal, but, at the time, I couldn't turn any in from a long way out.

We had a few passionate leaders that liked to call everything out and communicate. It made for many competitive games, and by being decently physical and not giving in to a charging offender, I earned the limited praise.

To be honest it was nice to have somewhere to be consistently, and you should have seen Nic play. In my opinion, he was at least the most fit if not the best player on the field.

He had a knack for scoring goals and both making and receiving long passes that made him a threat from almost anywhere when he touched the ball.

I felt privileged to watch him play. I admired Nic and wanted him to be better than me.

He put a lot of people to shame on the field, and not the least of which were some of the South Americans that played with us. Usually, there are a couple good ones, but I think that sometimes the pressure of being the one person from a country known for soccer gets you attention on the field from too many players.

We joked and played and traded stories on the sidelines. We had a good time. People from all over the world descended for these night games in Bangkok as if that certainty of a game made the experience all the more real.

For me, I enjoyed not really knowing anything about the group's organization. I just went with Nic who I think was part of a group chat, but for me it felt like we all just showed up because we were supposed to or like we had hoped something might happen.

That made the experience have some extended resonance that communicated a pious meaning. I could see that what we did brought us beyond the borders that had defined us before we came without changing us to make us any different from what we were as people before starting the game.

Despite the fact that I felt for a time like the loss of Mischa had cast some shroud of darkness over me, I could come here unannounced and be both expected and accepted.

It was reverential, but I also knew that I was going to leave, and often I would lay down on the ground after a game with Nic doing sit ups or bicycle kicks beside me thinking that we did indeed have it pretty good, but it would be nice to see how things had gotten along at home.

I feel like everyone felt similar in a way or at least that is what I hoped. In reality, there was no way of knowing if the place that they had come from would welcome them back the way that they were welcomed here.

Regardless of age or nationality, something could have kept them tied to Bangkok tighter than the loose strings that had broken for me with such an immature loss.

One time I played goalie and after making a few diving saves, the Englishmen who had seen a few American goalkeepers come across the pond joked that Americans did have a way with the position.

I've never been a good keeper since, so it must have gone straight to my head or something.

The field was far away from Nonsi, and so the trip was long. On the way back, we always stopped at a 7-Eleven to get drinks, and usually I would get this large basically two-liter thing of honey lemon green tea made by a Thai company named Oishi after the Japanese word for delicious.

Sweet, cold, and refreshing. I would drink it like water and fill up the empty container sometimes at Nonsi with this water dispenser on the second floor for a ten Baht coin.

Even though the fields were a far way off, there was not a place in Bangkok proper that cost more than eighty baht to get to by meter. Until we learned more about Bangkok taxis and how to navigate the negotiations, approaching drivers could be frustrating. They often started the bargain at one hundred or one fifty.

We would say "*meter khap*" and if they insisted, we'd shut the door and move on to the next car. Only the airports ever cost a bit to get out to, and it made things smoother to know a little bit about what we were getting into in terms of price and negotiations.

Irrational as it is, since you have to expect growing pains, there is seldom anything more embarrassing than allowing someone to hustle you out of some money.

People do it everywhere, and while I never really found the behavior disreputable, I'd much rather be known for being skeptical than to bend to the slightest flash of anything more circumstantial.

It's one of the reasons I rarely buy a girl a drink these days. I don't have much of a reason to. Plenty of my friends disagree with the strategy, but it depends on your intended results, I guess. Quality over quantity.

For example, Nic didn't date anyone or go around much in Thailand even though he's a good looking, nice guy. But he found someone when he came home, just the same. Maybe he envied the likes of Gerard who as a single man did a much better job cleaning up in the clubs, but he won out in the end, in my opinion. Not over Gerard, but for himself.

Everyone is different, and in a way the soccer field shed some light on the character of the individuals beyond their play. Nic took one good shot, once in a while, and usually made it while Gerard took a lot of shots and made more goals at a far lower percentage of success.

I honestly wonder what that says about me. Maybe it says more than I think. I guess you'd have to wonder if you think that I, or you, believe in anything I say.

• • •

Partly, I wanted to make this a cautionary tale. A tale of success as both a potential prelude to failure as well as not all that it is cracked up to be.

Even in "winning." Even in "succeeding." There is the possibility that you will never do enough to satisfy what truly wants ambition.

I can certainly think of enough examples much better than myself. Years of hard work may not let you leap beyond those things that seemingly held you back.

Some nights we had been classy, and some nights we had been less so. Finding a way to bridge the two in a night club and make a debut that didn't involve chasing the nearest girl's skirt seemed a necessity.

Nic helped me out with this one by bringing me along to one of his classmate's birthday parties at Escobar. I had been there for a birthday party before, which was a decently classy affair, but this upped the ante due to the class of the whole group.

There were no arguments between lovers. There were no drunken fits. Everything clicked even though there was something insane like twenty bottles of Johnnie Walker black label lined up on the table when I came in.

They just told me to drink. They didn't ask me for anything beyond that and my company. Nic introduced me to a few of the pretty Thai girls that he had gone to class with.

A pretty girl, who I think was there with her then boyfriend, now husband, and a few others. For some time afterwards, a few of us kept in touch.

We stood there sipping whiskey like we were gentleman and ladies, and we talked about things like the competitive strategies of the various banks in Thailand.

I have to say it was quite the departure from the norm, and probably what's come to be expected from me.

Certainly, I had been able to put a sentence or two together that could give some context. Yeah, we had in depth conversations plenty of times. They just usually happened at a nice, upper-class restaurant or over high tea. However, this was in one of the two buildings of Escobar. A place where I had walked through the ladies' bathroom less than a month before.

One of the times that I went with Finn, I had basically been a third wheel to his own invite. Another time I was there, I had basically spent the time on the smoker's deck, listening to Kristen while we plotted whether we were going to go to another club together.

Mundane, routine stuff. Certainly not whether flooding from the impending rainy season would affect banking operations in the region south and east of Bangkok due to their being prone to flooding.

I drank from the glass of whiskey, holding my own in conversation. I was at least able to impress someone with something other than my knowledge of fine dining or what makes for a good suit.

There was a pretty healthy guest list, which included some of members of the Thai Special Forces, and while neither of those two guys spoke any English, they seemed like good guys.

They also looked like they could throw a stone through a brick wall and kick a door off its hinges.

I kept the conversation to questions of overseas expansion and what challenges their company was facing.

No wonder Nic had spent most of his time with his own classmates, MBA students. Seeing us undergraduates running around in search of a cheap meal and a fast drink probably felt something like a middle schooler watching her little brother play at a day care when coming to pick him up. It's hard not to be waiting to leave.

Then again, if I've learned anything from reflecting on this whole experience, it is probably best to "be" an MBA when you're an MBA. Don't try to get too ahead of one's self or you might end up in over your head, but maybe that's part of the point to life. It's certainly hard to know one way or the other.

After Escobar, we went home.

It was one of the better times in Thailand, and it was just easy. I feel like if I was to go back or to live there, it was the type of experience that I would want to keep having.

Easy. Straight forward. Only the conversation needed to be complex.

And while there was a lot of complexity to how I could view the way that things unfolded, the only real complexity related to how to view or handle one's relationships.

To this day I haven't yet learned how best to tread that path, but I can tell you there is at least one thing that I wholeheartedly believe.

If one of the girls that you are speaking with is standing next to a member of the armed forces and he is trained to kill, you make sure to keep your eyes on her eyes and your hands at your sides.

I feel like that is pretty simple life advice.

It wasn't all professional soirees, however.

When it came time to renew my visa, I got a tip to take the gambler bus from Lumphini Park out to the Cambodian border.

Every morning at 6 a.m., a free bus would head out from there and take everyone out to the Cambodian border. There was a pair of casinos at the border in between the two countries. Gambling was illegal in Thailand, but this allowed people to get around it.

L led a contingent out there to the border at one point, and they had a blast. I had declined since I don't like to bet on anything but myself.

One night after hitting Khao San until five, at Mac's insistence, I boarded the bus to head out to the border in a vague state of fugue awareness.

I remember getting on the bus, but I was lucky that I had packed everything into a backpack before I left, because I was in bad shape.

I promptly fell asleep as the bus lurched forward, and I didn't even have time to ask any questions about destination or payment.

I hadn't even been drinking that much if at all. That particular night being after the whole Mischa thing, I had slowed down considerably.

Thankfully, there had been only the one bus, and it was the right bus. We ended up at the Cambodian border in somewhere between three and five hours I think. At first, when I checked my pockets, my phone and wallet were missing, but I found them underneath the seat.

No one was sitting behind me, so there was no one to have noticed them slip out of my stuff. The bus seats were like airplane seats, so I just had to feel around there with my hands and voila.

I climbed out of the bus assured that I didn't have to pay, and I ignored all the scammers standing out by the border. As I went through the customs exit, the only other guy in line was an Australian who did business in Phnom Penh and was on his way over for a spell.

He talked me through the customs process, which amounted to filling out a sheet of paper off to one side and handing it to the guy behind the counter with my passport.

That done, I had to argue that I had not overstayed my welcome for ten minutes before realizing that the customs official on my way into Bangkok the last time had not stamped my ticket with the morning I had arrived, but for the night before. A difference of about thirty minutes, but once this new guy had pointed me to the date on my visa, I was free to leave Thailand for a small fee.

I passed through the casinos, and I was surprised at how simple they looked. I had expected something on the gaudier side like Las Vegas, but they were more like two super stores out on the edge of nowhere.

I went into the Cambodian border and had no trouble with them. In Cambodia, I looked around, crossed the street, and went back in through an identical tunnel on the other side, which led back into Bangkok.

Coming back in at the same time was a tour group that included foreigners from a number of countries. I talked to a single Korean girl, who was the only one traveling alone.

Turns out she had been staying in Bangkok for some time and had gone on a trip to Cambodia on a whim. I asked her if I could join her on the way back to Bangkok, since I had neglected to figure out transportation back.

She agreed to help me out, and we grabbed lunch together and got the same van back. It was a pleasant ride, and she was a good conversationalist.

Neither of us seemed interested in anything more than being friendly, but she was cute and the transit time was so long that she ended up falling asleep in the van.

I got a window seat, and I stared out at the sun as we traveled that same, long highway I had taken back from Koh Chang only days before.

She yawned and rested her head on my shoulders. I thought better of disturbing her, and when the metropolitan sprawl of Bangkok came into view, I took a long last look at that exotic world that had changed me so much.

The long sun drifted into the reddish pink of the near-dusk pink shadows extended along the beige-brown, gray, and green of the city below. The same Bangkok night would come, I would see Nic and Talia again soon, and we would grab dinner together and relish in the simple fact that what had happened had happened. There was nothing else that we could ask for.

• • •

In the end, I guess the ending fit. What we truly had all along was merely hope. We could boil it all down to that. Hope that we could be more than what was there before us to take. That we made up the difference. That now the world would forever be a better place, because we were there to make it.

But, we cannot write over the past with the brushes of our own conscience. However, we may yearn to paint our own lives as those of the ones who overcame trials forever. With each little white lie to ourselves, which we may eternalize in memoir, we push the truth of the past back into the ether. That they were like us and just as misguided. Hopeful that they could make the difference before the storybook closed.

And what of us today? How do we compare? Can we not achieve something worthy of more than just the comment of someone else's idols?

We're fighting for the attention span of everyone. Only to realize that we were only entertaining ourselves. We all have the same ambition. We all believe that we are living a life that deserves some attention, but in that search, we seek the validation of other, more worthy sources.

Does it warrant the attention of anyone? The common thing is the thing that takes the longest time to build. All we truly need is time. Time to think. Time to understand, and it may take too much time for one to chase another through the trials of intellectual obscurity. Do I write then only to impress myself?

When I was younger, I was aware that I didn't know much, but I thought that I could at least know something. Truly, I know that I know nothing; not even the things that I know. Only then can I really have a chance of capturing anything true at all.

For what can I say about anything that's come that hasn't been said before? Some things remain the same. All we might achieve now is our own opportunity to build sand castles upon the ruins of those already strewn along the shore. The centuries have not always been kind to those who intend to offer more to the world than what was already there.

Take heart though, sweet child, for the chariot still rides across the sky each day with the fire of all Rome's gods in waiting. The very same brightness that stirred the emotions of all weary souls who ventured into the realms of the longing heart.

We seek to cast mountains in stone using only spit and the weeds that cropped up along on the strength of the rivers that bury the fountains of mystery in the temples of humanity's forgotten youth. It reverts the game to zero, sending the whole world into the shadow of the colossus.

We would toss out the wheel if we saw it. We would close Pandora's Box for fear that it might upset the status quo. And you wonder why the only "great" painters are dead. Are there no great artists? Or have we cast them asunder by our own hubris?

The truth is we've been played for fools. Learn what you must, but you'll never live up to your own shadow. That which lingers there in the echo of your own candle.

We should all ask: What makes us the ones who understand completely? We are all but figments of each other's and our own imaginations. Pawns in our own games and in those of others.

Doomed to hunger for the happiness of the ones that have walked the world before, but we might wonder always could I be happy for anything that comes? We tell each other sweet nothings, and it is the truth at the time.

The paltry existence of a sad mound of misshapen clay that defies the boundaries of some other. We fear what? The darkness?

Shadows merely fragmented to say what we might lose and which we've already disavowed with unmeasured gusto. Obsolescence, then? At the hands of what fate?

The future to many becomes a fate unto its own to more than you or I could count. We have nothing to fear save our own incapability of knowing when we must admit that we are going forward as what we are and have no more way to coax the future from its prison to warn our own hearts of certain doom than we have to alter the shape of the Hydrogen atom.

I implore us to seek questions for our answers and answers to our questions. Look for challenges beyond the epitome of yesterday and reaffirm the greatness of those who came before us, by questioning their singular ability to shed ample light where none may enter.

We attempt to find things that we hope are there rather than things that we know are not. Today we are taught to seek out our own paths to comfortable, achievable goals.

What was once basic education for children is now reserved for specific college disciplines. If we fail to respect that past completely, will we lose forward momentum?

Our basic instinct is to blot it out whether we are coached or not. That is the law, and it will remain the law until we give up our desire to have a singular truth.

And even in your questioning of others for your own fragile codes, you admit what you fail to challenge in yourself. The certainty that we cannot hold truth for ourselves.

Truth is beyond us. Unreachable. Unknowable. To find an answer is to only invite more questions. We know this, and yet we still pursue a corner of enigmatic singularity.

And so, we come at last upon the token meaning even if our search leads us to cower in fear of our self-awareness. How can we know if we have achieved anything at all or know if we've worked hard enough?

While we may not be able to ever find a singular truth, you can carve out something good for yourself, and if you do, keep it for yourself. Don't let anyone take it. The memory will make you happy, and there are times where people will try to make you suffer.

But if you've suffered before, you'll understand it when it comes, and you'll think of all the good your something has given you and know that something good will come again. And it will always come again.

This I know to be true.

About the Author

Christopher M. Struck enjoys writing contemporary and historical fiction. He is the author of *The Sun Never Set*, *Kennig & Gold*, and *8: A Song for the Peach Tree in My Master's Garden*.

He enjoys traveling, studying foreign languages, and is especially fond of the Japanese culture. He resides in New York City where he is working on his next book.

CPSIA information can be obtained
at www.ICGtesting.com
Printed in the USA
LVHW112108270922
729417LV00015B/337/J

9 781643 972800